POWER POSE

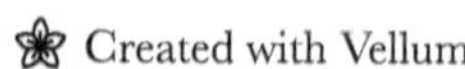 Created with Vellum

POWER POSE

EMILY SILVER

Love stories are more epic
with two heroines.
— Jordy Byrd

Author's Note

Power Pose was originally part of the Elite Connections LGBTQIA+ Anthology. It is now being published on its own with brand new content added.

Happy reading!
<3 Emily

Chapter One

RAVEN

"Do we have to go over it again?" the voice across the table whines. You'd think she was five instead of seventy-five.

"Gram, this is my very first conference with these girls. I want it to go off without a hitch."

She waves me off. "You're a badass businesswoman who runs the world before thirty. They're teenagers. They'll believe whatever you say."

"I'll tell them the sky is purple then and call it a day."

"I wouldn't go that far," she snickers.

"Then will you please help me?"

"Fine." She holds out her hand and I give her my note-cards. Adjusting her thick, oversized glasses, she assesses the cards. Her once brown hair is now completely gray. I hope I can age as gracefully as she has one day.

"Thank you."

"Why are you so nervous about this? You've made grown men cry."

Water spurts out of me over the mouthful I drank. "That was one time."

Her eyes are sparkling across from me. "And what a beautiful thing it was, darling. Weak men couldn't handle a woman like you."

"Then it's a good thing I don't need a man."

Taking off her glasses, Gram pierces me with a knowing stare. And because this isn't the first time we've had this conversation, I know exactly what is coming.

"You haven't met a nice young lady, have you?"

"I told you, I'm not really looking right now."

"You're not getting any younger, Raven."

"I know." She tells me this every time we get together now it seems. "Most people don't get married now until later."

"Your mother was ten years old by the time I was your age!" she nags.

"If I tell you I'll try, would you at least drop it? For now?"

"Telling me you'll try and actually doing it are two different things, darling. Don't think I don't know how you're playing this."

Nothing gets by my Gram.

When I moved to Seattle for college to be closer to my grandparents, I never imagined I would take over their business.

Sure, I wanted to follow in their footsteps and work for West Investments, but I never thought I would be the CEO.

I thought I would have more of a life before that happened.

Now, work is my life.

"If you don't find someone soon, I might have to resort to setting up your dating profile."

My jaw drops. "You wouldn't dare," I finally say.

"Hmm, I like this idea." She ignores me. "Who

wouldn't want a catch like you? Good hips and nice eyes. Personality could use some work. Other than that, you'd be any woman's dream. Maybe there's a working women dating app I could find for you."

"Hey, personality does not need work!" I balk.

"I love you, dear, but work can't be everything if you want to settle down."

"If you want me to settle down, then why would you use a working women app for me?"

Gram waves me off. "You're right. That makes you sound like a hooker. Nothing wrong with that, but you're not."

Not how I saw this conversation going. "Gram. I have to go. I need to get back to the office and do some things before the conference tonight."

"Sure, sure." She waves at me like I'm interrupting her day.

"I love you." I drop a quick peck on her cheek. "Don't you dare set a dating profile up for me. You haven't heard the end of this."

"Love you, dear."

I pay the bill on the way out and call for a rideshare to get back to the office. No use in trying to find a cab when it's another rainy, summer day. Answering emails on the way back to work, I can't help but think about Gram's words.

It's not like I'm *not* trying to find someone. It's just that no one wants to date someone who works eighteen hours a day.

My company demands it.

I love what I do.

When I took over West Investments, I overhauled the kinds of companies we bought and supported.

Small businesses.

Women-owned.

Minority-owned.

I wanted everyone to feel supported, no matter their background. It's how I was raised. With two loving parents and two sets of grandparents, I never had to worry about coming out to them.

It's my small way of paying it forward.

Getting back to the office, I wave to the security officer and take the elevator straight up to the top floor.

Everything is sleek and modern. Light gray walls with pink and teal accents. Hardwood floors give it a warm feel when you step inside our offices. Floor-to-ceiling windows with a view of the sound greet me, but today it's hard to see anything except fog and rain.

"How are things here?" I drop my phone in my bag and take the file from my assistant, Chelsea. No doubt she was awaiting my arrival.

"Are you ready for the good news?" She's vibrating with excitement as she follows me to my corner office.

"What?"

"That company you've been eyeing? TraveLLin'? It's up for sale."

"Wait, really?" I open the folder she gave me, and right there in black and white is the information for the company I've been dreaming about.

"It looks like the owner and her wife are wanting to retire."

My eyes fly across the page. The company's history, finances, everything…it's all outlined right there for potential buyers.

"I can't believe this is real."

There's no way I heard her right.

"See for yourself." She taps a few things on her iPad and hands it over to me.

There, on their social media page is a long post about how the owner is ready to enjoy a slower pace of life. It's a sentimental post. Talking about how she met her partner and how she grounded her while she spent most of her days at the office or traveling the world.

"Isn't it cute how she came up with the name traveL-Lin'?" Chelsea asks, a wistfulness to her voice. Her amber eyes are soft as she tucks a pen into the blonde bun sitting on top of her head. *So she doesn't lose them* she once told me.

"The two L's for lesbian?" I smile back at her. It's well documented how she named the company when she fell in love with her wife.

Normally, I'd enjoy the sappy side of a business.

But I'm trying to absorb all this information as best I can.

Because there is no way I'm going to lose this.

"Do you have any more information? Are they meeting with potential buyers?"

"Hang on."

Chelsea takes the iPad back from me and starts tapping into some files.

The company I've dreamed about owning since I first found out about it. An LGBTQIA+ company that specializes in safe travel around the world for people like me.

When I first discovered it in college, I was planning a backpacking trip with my girlfriend at the time and loved everything they had. Places to go, things to avoid. Everything about it called to me.

If I wasn't already set to follow in the family business, I would've worked there.

Except the company is based in Milan. And there was no way that I would've gotten my girlfriend to move there after college.

"Okay. There's an attachment here regarding the sale."

Strutting around my glass desk, I hover over her shoulder, reading the information.

"Good." I point to something on the screen. "We'll have that initial capital. Get the rest of the paperwork in order tomorrow. I'm not going to lose this because we're twiddling our thumbs."

"I know." Chelsea has a huge grin on her face. "Trust me, boss. I will do everything I can to make sure this deal happens for you."

"God, I need something to drink."

"Here." Chelsea hands me the tablet and heads to the drink cart in the corner.

The Seattle sky beyond the windows is starting to turn a dark gray. I normally love this time of year.

The cool breeze coming off the sound makes the summer days bearable, but we're going through a rainy spell.

Except nothing can ruin my day today.

"Drink."

The iced tea slides down my throat, settling my nerves as I read over the sale information.

Until my eyes latch on to one piece of information.

"Shit."

"What's wrong?" Chelsea asks.

"There. The last paragraph."

"Eden Sands is looking to invite potential buyers and their partners to an event in Milan prior to the sale. Eden is looking to sell traveLLin' to a well-rounded businessperson that understands the delicate nature of a work-life balance."

"So you take a girlfriend? What's the big deal?"

"Big deal?" My voice gets loud as my head snaps around to face her. "In case you haven't noticed, I don't have one."

"Well…you could…how about…"

She taps a manicured finger against her lips, trying to brainstorm.

The one thing I've always wanted is so close I can taste it. There's no way I'm going to let some other person snatch this company out from under me because I don't have a partner.

I will do whatever it takes to get this company.

Fuck. Almost anything.

Maybe Gram was on to something.

Except, how the hell am I going to find someone to be my girlfriend in the next week?

Chapter Two

"Do you have the case files for the Riley case?"

"Which Riley case? I have two."

"Insurance fraud."

Shuffling the towering stack of files around on my desk, I hand the right file to the prosecutor. "This is everything I have so far."

"Thanks, Blair. We should be heading to trial with this one within the week."

"Keep me updated. I'm ready for this one to be over with."

"So you can focus on all your other cases?" My boss laughs.

"All thirty of them."

Life as an assistant prosecutor. The good work is never done. As soon as one case is crossed off the docket, another five land on my plate. No matter what I do, I can never get ahead on the cases I have.

Yet, it's still better than being a junior associate for a big firm. I couldn't handle the hours. Not with needing to be home more often.

Law books the size of bricks take up one side of my desk while the chaotic pile of papers is strewn across the always messy surface.

The buzzing of my phone on my desk pulls my attention away from the files that threaten to collapse on top of me.

My sister's high school.

This can't be good.

Tension bunches my shoulders. I haven't even picked up and I know I'm not going to like this call.

"This is Blair Stevens."

"Miss Stevens. This is secretary Wilson from Avi's school."

"Is everything okay?"

"Avi has been suspended—"

"Suspended?" I cut her off. "For what?"

"For breaking the dress code."

I can picture her prim face screwing up at my sister breaking the dress code for some minor infraction.

"You will need to come pick her up and meet with the assistant principal. She can return to school on Wednesday."

Almost a week from now. We can't even get a break during summer school. Avi wants to be done with high school as much as I do and is taking classes during the holiday break to get ahead.

"Wednesday? That seems drastic."

Fuck. This is the last thing I need to deal with right now. With court next week, I won't be able to be home with Avi.

"I will be there shortly, Miss Wilson."

"We'll see you then."

She hangs up without another word. Grabbing everything I need to work from home for the afternoon, I let my boss know I'm leaving and head out.

A steady rain is coming down now as I leave the Seattle court building.

Great. Digging in my bag for my umbrella, I come up empty.

You'd think I'd be used to this by now. It's even better because I'm in a pair of heels that aren't made for running.

By the time I cross the parking lot to my old, but trusty, car, I look like a drowned rat.

I blow out a breath, pulling back my blonde hair into a haphazard bun. The rearview mirror doesn't do anything to help my look. Mascara is caked under my eyelashes and my eye shadow is smeared.

I do my best to clean myself up before I leave for Avi's school.

Taking care of my little sister is the last thing I planned on doing, but I wouldn't change it for the world. Even for all the headaches she causes me.

Or the headaches that aren't her fault.

I was lucky to get her into the school she's in. It's one of the best schools in Seattle and I know she's getting a good education. With a recommendation from my boss, it was all but a guarantee.

But I hate the administration. It seems no matter what line Avi toes, she's always getting called into the principal's office.

It makes doing my job hard, but thankfully I have an understanding boss.

By the time I make it across the city at this time of day, I'm a little less wet. Damp clothes stick to me as I grab the umbrella in my car and head into the office.

And there's the little troublemaker now. She's a mini

version of me. Long blonde hair and bright blue eyes. Except for the curves. She's as gangly as a stick.

"You okay, Avi?" I ask.

She's dressed in a dark zip-up hoodie and jeans, so I'm having a hard time finding what dress code violation she broke.

Did they really call me out of work to come get her for this?

"I'm fine," she grumbles. She picks at a spot on her jeans. Jeans that I had to shell out a pretty penny for in order to make sure they met the dress code. One rip above the knee and it would be detention. "Fascists trying to tell me what to wear."

She grabs her backpack, and I take the paperwork handed to me by the secretary without comment. God, what I wouldn't give to lay into them.

"I'm really sorry, Blair," Avi tells me once we're outside of the building.

"It's not your fault."

"Yes, it is."

"It's this stupid school's fault," I grumble, getting back into the car. "Listen, let's grab some Dick's on the way home."

"I get suspended and you suggest Dick's? I thought I was in trouble."

"Hey, might as well make the most of it."

Because if she's going to be stuck at home for the next week, I can worry about dinner tomorrow.

All of the same problems will still be there. Nothing is ever going to be easy for the two of us. But at least this can be.

A bag of Dick's always makes things better.

Chapter Three

RAVEN

"We're doomed."

"How can you have a defeatist attitude like that?"

I grab a fry and drag it through the ketchup before chomping down on it. "The invitation says Raven West and partner. And in case you haven't noticed, Chelsea"—I pierce my assistant with a knowing look across the desk—"I haven't had a girlfriend in over two years."

"Okay, so a minor inconvenience."

I fight the eye roll and grab another fry, trying to rack my brain for any possible solution. Now that I finally have the chance to buy the company, I don't want my single status to stop me.

"And where do you suggest I find a girlfriend to leave for an event that starts next week?" I point a finger at her. "And don't say you, because I don't want to face Cora's wrath."

Chelsea screws up her face. "I wasn't even going to suggest myself as an option. You couldn't pay me enough."

"Ouch." I grab my strawberry shake and take a hearty

gulp. Nothing like a little reality check that you're not everyone's type.

Exactly why you're in this situation, Raven.

Even when I was dating, I was too picky. No one met the high standards I set. I got bored too easily. It seemed everyone was more interested in my job—and the dollar signs that came with it—than in me. Instead of worrying about dating, my work became my life. Not that I minded, because I love what I do.

Except for the part where we've been sitting around the conference room table for hours trying to figure out how this is going to work.

Chelsea's eyes widen. "Hold on. There is something…"

"What?" I lean across the desk, needing any scrap of information that could potentially help me look like a well-rounded person.

Their words, not mine. I'm a well-rounded person without a partner, thank you very much.

"Another assistant was talking about how their boss used this company to find him the type of person he needed."

"Like an escort service?" Sounds like the dating app my Gram had in mind for me.

She waves me off. "No. If you have a certain need that needs fulfilled, like hiring a nanny or someone to take to an event with you, they can provide you that."

"What's it called?"

"Elite Connections."

"I've never heard of them."

A coy smile spreads across Chelsea's face. "I doubt you have. I only know about it because of the assistants' network."

"And would they be able to find me someone… suitable?"

She nods, practically gleeful. "Yes. I have their info and we can message them."

She pops up from her spot and runs out to her desk with surprising ease for wearing a pencil skirt and stiletto heels.

Hire someone to be my girlfriend? It's crazy. Probably one of the craziest things I've ever done.

But I want this more than anything. If I have to hire someone to play the part—to pretend to be in love with me—it's worth it.

"Here you go."

Chelsea slaps a sticky note with an email address on it down on my desk.

"This is it?" I hold the pink paper up in my hands.

contact@eliteconnections.com

"How do I know this isn't some teenage boy trying to swindle people out of money?"

Chelsea rolls her eyes at me. "Are you really going to doubt the assistants' network?"

"No," I grumble.

"Then email them. The sooner the better, otherwise you get charged more."

Leaning back in her chair, Chelsea looks like this is all but guaranteed.

One little email address with the power to change my future.

"And just tell them, what, I need a girlfriend?"

"Yes. Email them and they'll take care of the rest."

Still wary, I open my email, type out their address, and tell them what I need.

"This feels desperate," I tell her as I hit send.

"Aren't you, though?"

"I don't want them to know that." I drop my phone on my desk and suck down the last of my shake.

"It's why they're there if you need them." Chelsea nods. "They only work on recommendations. If you don't have someone who worked with them, you won't find them. It's for people like you."

"People like me?" I quirk a brow.

"People who have money and can spend it. You pay a premium for the service to get what you need."

"So a girlfriend for the next three weeks?"

"Exactly."

My email dings within minutes.

Good evening Ms. West,

Thank you for contacting Elite Connections. We here at Elite pride ourselves on matching our exclusive clientele with whatever they may need. Our aim is to match your desires and exceed your expectations.

In order to best match you, please take some time to fill out the information below, and we will match you with a suitable partner.

If assistance is needed within twenty-four hours, please contact us at the number below.

Should you accept our services, a separate email with wire instructions will be sent for payment.

Thank you for reaching out! It is our pleasure to serve you here at Elite Connections.

Holy shit.

"They responded."

"Not a teenage boy?"

I smirk at her. "No."

"Let me see." Chelsea steps around the desk and pulls the phone out of my hand. "Wow, they are detailed.

Height. Weight. They even ask what college you would prefer they attended."

"Why are you shocked by this?" I grab the phone and go back to looking at the questions. There have to be two hundred questions on this thing.

"It seems like it would be hard to pair you with someone at that level of detail."

"Are you saying I'm too picky?"

Chelsea mimes zipping her lips and heads back around the desk. "On that note, I am going home to my wife."

"See if I give you your Christmas bonus then."

Chelsea waves over her shoulder. "Raven, this place would go up in flames without me." She's right, but I don't tell her that. "I expect a trip to Tahiti once you seal that deal with traveLLin'."

She leaves me in peace to fill out the questionnaire.

Question after question. The farther I get down the list, the more I'm starting to question my sanity. I've never done anything like this in my life.

Am I really going to do this?

I answer each question as best I can, trying not to get overwhelmed by it all. Knowing I'll full well do what I need to in order to make this happen.

I hit submit.

No going back now.

Chapter Four

BLAIR

"Look who finally surfaces!" Sarina wraps me in a hug. A cool breeze is blowing in off the sound. It's a warm, July day, but comfortable with the wind.

"Excuse me if I've been in court all week." I drop my bag onto the bench beside me.

"How's the case?" She hands me a brown bag, and I take the empty seat on the bench next to her.

"Should be wrapped up by the end of next week." I open the bag, inhaling the sweet scent of pho. "This smells amazing."

"You look starved."

"I am. God, I hate being in court and eating PB&J."

"I figured. Good thing I had to be down here to file some paperwork."

"How is your big case going?" I blow on the broth before shoveling another bite in my mouth.

"If I leave the office before ten, it's a good day."

One of the reasons I left the private firm I was working at during my last year in law school—there was no way I could work there and take care of Avi.

"At least you look good while doing it."

I've known Sarina since law school. She's one of the only people I can see on a regular basis because she butts her way in. In the most loving of ways, of course.

No matter how busy she is with work, she always looks dressed to the nines. Designer suits and shoes. Name-brand handbags.

One of the perks of that private firm.

Meanwhile, my public office paycheck gets me a secondhand suit and sensible pumps. Everything else I have goes toward Avi's school.

"Maybe I should send you home with some of my suits. Then she won't be breaking the dress code."

"Oh God," I groan, pushing my sunglasses higher up on my nose. The sun feels good after being stuck in my office all day. "I'm sure they'd find something wrong with them."

"Why do you send her to that horrible school?"

"Because it's the best of the best."

"Where she'll become a little snotty zombie who only wears power suits."

"As long as she graduates."

Sarina waves me off. "She'll graduate and then head to law school just like you."

"God, I hope not."

"You don't want her following in your footsteps?" Sarina crosses a leg, leaning back on the bench. Pink colors her cheeks from the sun.

"Not if I can help it. Maybe art school."

"About as far from law as you can get."

"Absolutely."

We catch up over our bowls of noodles. The noises of Seattle rage behind us. Ferry boats are coming and going.

It's one of the many reasons I chose to stay in Seattle

after school. I love the energy here. Even though I don't get to enjoy it, I love the pulse of the city. There's never a dull moment.

My email pings in my coat pocket. I groan, not wanting to cut lunch short. But the email that pops up is one I never thought I would see.

"Holy shit."

"What?" Sarina peeks over my bowl, looking at my phone. "What is it?"

"Do you remember that Elite Connections agency you hooked me up with?"

"Was that them?"

"Yup." I pop the *p*, eyes straining to focus on the email.

"I didn't think you'd heard from them."

"Not since you convinced me to apply."

It was an impulse one drunken night. Sarina knew about this place from a friend of a friend. They look for people with certain skills that can easily blend into events where those skills are needed. The paycheck that came with attending these events was something that also drew me in.

I don't know how I was ever vetted, but I'm guessing it has to do with my law degree.

"What do they want?"

"They need me for a few weeks to be someone's girlfriend."

My eyes flit over the screen trying to lock on to important details. But the only thing they can focus on is the payment fee.

"Am I looking at all those zeros right?" I shove my sunglasses onto the top of my head to make sure I'm looking at it right. I show the screen to Sarina. "There's no way I'm looking at that number correctly."

"Holy shit." She grabs my phone, counting the numbers. "Do you know how much money that is?"

"Give me my phone back."

I steal it from the clutches of her grip.

"That much money…"

"Could pay for Avi's school, college, and pay off all your student loans?"

I swallow around the lump in my throat.

"Well, mostly. Law school wasn't cheap."

"But still. Isn't your biggest worry Avi's school?"

"She wouldn't have to worry about school at all."

"Then why are you even thinking about this? You have to do it."

"Says who?" I put my phone down, trying to erase those zeros from my mind.

"Me." Sarina grabs my bowl and puts the lid on it, setting it to the side. "You are the most even-keeled person I've ever met. Nothing gets to you. Taking in your sister? You didn't think twice. Changing jobs? No big deal to you. So why are you hesitating on this?"

"I can't just leave Avi for a few weeks to go to…" I grab my phone, looking at the detailed itinerary. "Oh my God."

"Where?" Sarina's eyes lock on mine.

"Italy. Milan."

"Are you serious?"

I nod, trying not to let myself get excited about this.

"A few weeks in Milan? It's the one place you've always wanted to go."

God, it really is. I had grand plans of traveling all across Europe after I graduated law school. Instead, I ended up with Avi on my doorstep and started working for the King County Prosecutor.

"What about Avi? I can't just leave her."

"Easy. She can stay with me."

"Just like that?"

"Just like that. Blair. For once in your life, don't weigh the pros and cons. You'll talk yourself out of this. You need this. Something just for you. And that paycheck. It'd let you have some breathing room for once."

My brain is spinning. Every single dollar that comes in is accounted for each month. There's no wiggle room. Flat tire? I'd have to take the bus to work in order to save to fix it.

That much money could make things easier for me. For both of us.

Could I really do this? Every single thing I've done since Avi ended up with me has been for her. I've had only a handful of days where I did something just for me.

"Well…"

A smile paints Sarina's face. "That sounds like a positive well…"

"If you can watch Avi, and I can get the time off work. Then…I guess I'm going to Italy."

Chapter Five

BLAIR

"**A**re you sure you know what you're doing?" Sarina asks, pulling up to the curb.

"Yes. I know exactly what I'm doing."

"Then why do you keep doing that?" She nods to where my fingers are picking at the hem of my sweater.

I put on my best outfit. My favorite. The one that always makes me feel like I can take on the world. An over-sized white button-up dress with a fitted black sweater over it and low-heeled black booties.

I need to look the part, right?

I've only thought about it every minute of the last few days.

"I'll be fine once I meet her."

Sarina throws the car into park and turns to face me. "Why haven't you met this woman yet?"

"Raven," I clarify.

"Fine, why haven't you met *Raven* yet?"

"I had two days before leaving. It was more important to get Avi taken care of."

"Is this your way of asking me if I'll be okay with her?"

I laugh, pushing open the car door to grab my bags.

"No. You're about the only person she'll listen to, so she's fine."

"Are you including yourself in that?"

Sarina comes around and pops the trunk to her black sports car.

"Yes. No one likes being told what to do."

"And yet, you'll have to do exactly what's asked of you for the next few weeks."

I roll my eyes and heft my bag out of the trunk. It's small. I packed the essentials and a few nicer things, not quite knowing what all we'd be doing while there.

I was given a basic itinerary, being told to plan for the unexpected. It took everything I had not to cancel then and there. I hate the unexpected. I like order in my life. It means I don't have to worry.

"It'll be fine."

"You know you don't have to have sex with this person, right?"

"Jesus, Sarina." I love my best friend, but sometimes I wonder why. "Trust me, I know."

"Good. And you were able to get the time off work?"

"I work in the prosecutor's office. I'll be fine."

I haven't taken a single sick day in all the time I've worked there. I had to plead my case, but with all the job openings they have, I'm not really concerned about my position.

Between the debts I have and paying to get Avi through school, I would be an idiot to pass this up. Anything to try and make our lives easier.

"I can't believe you're going to Milan," Sarina sighs. "I wish I could go to Italy."

"I'll be sure to send you a postcard."

"I'd hate you if I didn't love you so much."

I laugh, trying to settle the nerves inside me.

I was told to meet Raven here at the bag check. I don't see anyone that is on their own who could be her.

"You should probably get going."

"Worried she'll take one look and want me instead?" She waggles her brows at me.

"Yes. That's exactly it," I deadpan. "Now go."

"Call me if you need me. Love you!"

"I will. Love you."

Sarina gets into her car and drifts off into the melee of airport traffic. My eyes go back to scanning the airport for the woman I'm going to be spending this trip with. The details of the arrangement between us were in depth. All the information I would need to make it through this trip.

To Milan.

The one place in the world I've wanted to go as long as I can remember. But couldn't because of the crushing weight of my responsibilities.

"Cheating on me already?"

Spinning on my heel, my jaw drops.

"Raven?"

This is the woman I'll be spending the next few weeks with?

The dark-haired beauty is stunning. There's no other way to describe her. An absolute bombshell.

"That would be me."

She extends her hand to me. Almond-shaped nails are bright red. Olive skin. Dark black hair. A beauty mark that sits right above her plump lips. Curves for days.

She embodies every bit of her name. Raven.

"And you're Blair?"

I give her a shy smile and nod. "Otherwise that would make this very awkward."

Dark eyes give me an assessing once-over. I shift under her gaze.

I didn't have much time to do a lot of digging into her. Sure, I got a full breakdown on her from Elite, but that doesn't tell me much about her as a person. And an Internet search will only get you so far.

"Then I'm glad I picked the right woman out of the crowd."

"You didn't have my photo ahead of time?" I quirk a brow at her.

"Maybe."

Her pictures that I found online did not do her justice.

My love life these last few years? Nonexistent. Raising a teenage girl on my salary? There's no way I had any time for anything other than worrying about Avi.

Raising a teenager is like dealing with a moody toddler every day…who can drive.

But maybe if the dating pool included someone like Raven, I would've been more keen to get back out there.

"Are you ready to leave?"

Raven stirs me from my thoughts as I follow her to the bag drop.

For someone who is about to board a ten-plus hour flight, Raven looks stunning. Black ankle pants, a black, deep V-neck silk shirt, and a caramel trench jacket with red-soled stilettos. With the name-brand bag, she's the epitome of polished CEO.

Even if I was up for dating, Raven is so far out of my league, it's not even funny. If we met at some bar, she wouldn't look twice at me.

We drop our bags and make it through security without issue. With traffic getting to the airport, boarding starts any minute.

"So you're the one that's going to be my girlfriend for the next few weeks?"

"That's me." I try to instill more confidence in my voice than I'm feeling.

Raven laughs, a smooth sound like a glass of red wine sliding down your throat. "Never been hired to be someone's fake girlfriend?"

"Can't say that I have."

"If it helps, I've never hired anyone either. Better than my Gram trying to set me up on a dating site."

"Your Gram has a vested interested in your sex life?"

"She wants me to be as happy as she is."

"Ah."

I go to ask her why she hired me, but the boarding announcement cuts me off.

"Good evening, everyone, and welcome to Italian Air Flight Three with service to Milan. We would like to welcome our pre-boards at this time and anyone who might need extra time to board."

Raven switches her oversized bag to the other arm and shifts to face me. "You're not a nervous flier, are you?"

"No. It's been awhile since I've flown, but turbulence doesn't bother me."

"Good."

"Our first class and Millionaire Milers are welcome to board."

People are crowded around the gate, waiting to board.

"That's us."

"First class?" My jaw drops, for the second time tonight. I have a feeling it's going to be something that keeps happening around her. Raven had the tickets through security, so I didn't think twice about where we'd be sitting.

Raven's lips quirk up in a smile. "I wanted to get to

know you better without all the curious ears of every person on this flight."

I follow her down the empty jet bridge, trying to wrap my head around everything that's happened these last few days. And what is going to happen over the course of these next few weeks.

This isn't my life.

A first class flight to Milan?

No one pinch me because I don't want to wake up from this dream.

Especially with Raven at my side.

Shit. I shouldn't be thinking of waking up next to Raven. That would only complicate matters. And my life is complicated enough.

We're greeted by a flight attendant and a glass of champagne as we find our seats. Wide, cushy seats with oversized TVs take up the first class area. A dopp kit, pillow, and fluffy blanket await us.

Setting my drink down, I heft my bags into the overhead bin and take my seat.

"Wow. This is really nice."

Raven drops down next to me. I've never sat in anything so nice on a plane before.

"Here's to enjoying the next ten hours together then."

She holds her glass up and I clink mine against hers.

The cool bubbles help calm the nerves that are still floating through me. The cabin is quiet up here as people board behind us.

"Can I ask why you needed to hire me?" I sip on the champagne as the flight attendants finish their preflight checks. "I can't wrap my head around the fact that you couldn't find someone on your own."

Raven laughs, leaning over the small divider between our seats.

"Meaning what?"

I groan, knocking back the rest of my drink. "Are you really going to make me say it?"

"Yes."

I love how direct she is. No wonder she became a CEO of her own company before she turned thirty.

"You're gorgeous. I have a hard time believing you're not dating some supermodel from Brazil."

"That would require me going to Brazil to get a supermodel."

"Fine. Then a supermodel in Seattle."

"Not my type," she answers quickly. Almost too quickly.

"No? Then what is your type?"

"I'm really not picky." Her eyes shift, roving over my exposed legs. Heat gathers between my legs at her slow perusal. "Contrary to what my Gram thinks."

I should not be having these kinds of feelings for her. It's been a long time since I've felt like this. But this is a job. One that will pay me handsomely by the time I get home.

It shouldn't be this hard to be her fake girlfriend, right?

"Tell me about yourself." Raven stirs my thoughts.

"What do you want to know?"

"Anything. Everything. We've been dating for a year—"

I laugh, cutting her off. "Only a year?"

She taps one of her perfectly manicured fingers on my forearm. "I figure that's a good amount of time to bring someone on a trip like this. But not long enough that people will question why we're not married."

I roll my eyes. "Not that it's anyone's business but ours, but you're right."

"You're an attorney, right?" Raven asks, getting another glass of champagne for each of us from the passing flight attendant.

"Assistant prosecutor. About as far down on the food chain as you can get."

"You sound like you don't like it."

I snort. "That's putting it mildly."

"Why did you go into law then?"

I circle a finger over the rim of my glass. "Money. Prestige. But then my sister came to live with me and I couldn't work the long hours of a junior associate. So I left my firm and went to work for the prosecutor's office."

"Wow. That's dedication. Why did you take in your sister?"

"Off-limits." My tone is clipped. It's the one topic I don't want to discuss with people.

She throws her hands up. "Okay. Tell me something easier then."

Raven doesn't back down. A lesser woman would've curled into her seat and let me be. I like this about her. That she doesn't let me crawl back into myself at the painful memories.

"I love soccer."

"Playing or watching?"

"Watching. I have zero athletic ability. Atlanta Rising is my club."

"Your club?" Raven lifts a perfectly groomed brow at me.

"I take it you're not a soccer fan."

"Not at all. Explain it to me."

The plane backs up from the gate and heads down the runway before soaring into the darkening Seattle skies as I tell her about my favorite sport. If the entire flight is going to be like this, I wouldn't mind one minute.

Raven West is someone I want to get to know.

"I feel like you need to watch a game with me for me to

understand all of that. I maybe understand half of our football."

"I will explain it to you then. It's easy enough to understand."

"I'll be the judge of that." Raven kicks off her shoes and pulls her legs up onto her seat as the plane levels off. "Favorite food?"

"Nue is my favorite restaurant."

"Really?"

I nod, cracking open the water bottle at my seat. "I like that I can travel without leaving Seattle."

"Is that what you're passionate about?"

"As passionate as one can be when they can't leave the city."

A sly smile slides onto her face. "Filing that away for later."

What later she's talking about, I don't know.

"What about you? What's your favorite food?"

"Dick's."

"I'm sorry?" I choke over my water, my eyes nearly bugging out of my head.

"Dick's burgers. Tell me you've had them."

"I just can't believe you have. It's my sister's favorite."

"They are the best. Whenever I work late, it's the best to get me through. Their strawberry shakes are to die for."

"Aren't you full of surprises? Who would've thought you'd like a bag of Dick's?"

She matches my stance, inching closer. "Oh yes. Nothing I love more than an entire bag of Dick's. I love eating them."

"I'm sure you do."

"All the time."

"Umm, I'm sorry to interrupt,"—the flight attendant

looks thoroughly shocked—"but are you ready for your meals?"

"Yes," Raven answers without taking her eyes off me. "It'll be no bag of Dick's…"

Being under her stare—being her sole focus—has me squirming in my seat. I take it back. If this is the entire flight, I don't know if I'll make it.

Raven West is going to be the end of me.

Chapter Six

RAVEN

"You ready for all of this?" The car pulls to a stop in front of the hotel. White stucco buildings with big black awnings welcome us in. Milan passed by us in a blur from the airport to the city center.

A mix of modern and historical buildings are scattered everywhere.

"Does it matter if I am?" Blair steps out of the car, wide eyes taking in everything around her.

Milan is bustling all around us. People coming and going to the main square just a short distance from our hotel. Flowering trees line the street.

I pull Blair to the side as a bellboy dressed in an impeccable suit grabs our bags. "If you're going to have a freak-out, I'd prefer you do it now rather than inside."

A lazy smile spreads across Blair's face. She holds her hand up between us. Steady. Even. "No nerves. I've got this."

That makes one of us.

After in-flight delays, we arrived much later than I

wanted. We won't have much time to get ready for the cocktail hour tonight.

"I will be the perfect doting partner. I can give you the entire history of this company from front to back."

"You can?" I raise a questioning brow in her direction.

"TraveLLin' was founded in 1980 by Eden Sands. Since then, it's become one of the most well-known LGBTQIA+ companies in the world. Each year, twenty percent of profits are given to charities around the world supporting their mission."

Holy shit.

As if I already wasn't attracted to Blair. The minute I saw her in the airport, there was a pull there.

We spent the majority of the flight talking. I wanted to know everything I could about her. No fact was too small.

There's something about her, though, that is closed off. I want to peel back those layers and get to know her.

But it's not for me to learn.

She's here these next few weeks to try and help me win over Eden and buy traveLLin'.

Hearing her spout off facts, though, about traveLLin' like she's done her due diligence on the company?

Competence porn is a real thing.

"Wow. You weren't kidding."

Blair leans in close, her lips ghosting the shell of my ear. A shudder racks my body. "I'm a research nerd. I love learning everything I can for situations like this."

"I'm glad you're by my side," I tell her truthfully.

Anyone else and we would probably be made within minutes.

"I will do everything in my power to make sure you get this company, Raven. I promise."

"Then let's do this."

Linking hands with her, I walk us through the lobby to

the check-in desk. Our heels clack on the marble tiled floors. A fireplace sits empty on one wall with couches situated around it. Behind the check-in desk, a courtyard is bustling with guests grabbing drinks. Groups of tourists are crowded around maps, planning their day in the city, their excited voices echoing off the arched ceilings.

It's everything a European hotel should be.

"Buongiorno! Welcome to Milan. Are you checking in?"

"Yes." I give the receptionist a big smile and pull out my ID and credit card for him.

"Ahh, Miss West. It's a pleasure to have you joining us for the next few weeks."

"We've never been to Milan. We're looking forward to it."

"You will love our fine city. So much to do and see." He gives us a grin and a nod as he taps away on his keyboard. "We have you in our most luxurious king suite."

"King? As in one bed?" Blair asks, her gaze snapping to meet mine.

I give Blair a syrupy smile. "What's wrong with that, honeybunch? You don't want to snuggle?"

I burrow into her side as she tries to fight a grimace. "Nothing wrong with that."

"With how booked we are for the convention, we had to upgrade you in order to accommodate your request for the suite," the receptionist tells us.

"Thank you. It sounds wonderful."

He smiles back at her, punching away on his keyboard before handing over two keys. "The elevator is at the end of the lobby on your right. If there is anything we can do to make your stay more enjoyable, please let us know."

"Grazie."

The wheels of our bags click along the tile in the lobby as we head in the direction he pointed us.

"Honeybunch? Really?" Blair asks, crossing her arms the minute we step into the elevator. Her stern look is echoed through the mirrored car. As if endless Blairs are disapproving of the situation we just landed ourselves in.

"Not a fan of nicknames, schnookums?"

She bursts out laughing, a sweet sound that hits me square in the chest.

Get it together, Raven. You're paying her to be here. If you weren't, you wouldn't even be here right now.

"Would you be, cookie?" she throws back at me.

"Touché."

I study her. The way the hem of her dress flutters around her thighs. All that blonde hair of hers is swept up on top of her head. After spending more than a dozen hours on the plane, she looks just as stunning as when she stepped on it.

Her cerulean-blue eyes are studying me just as carefully. I wonder what she thinks when she looks at me.

The elevator doors open, pushing us out to the top floor of the hotel, where there are two doors. Finding ours, I wave the keycard over the lock as the green light clicks.

"Wow." Blair's jaw drops as she takes in the expansive room.

Black-and-white wallpaper is accented by oversized green furniture. Gold lamps sit on the tables in the living room. Old portraits of models hang on the walls. A door to the bedroom sits off to the left, and ahead of us, French doors open onto the terrace with stunning views of Milan and the Duomo. With only a small set of table and chairs, it's the perfect spot for morning coffee.

It's more modern than I thought it would be for a hotel in Milan.

"Is it weird I thought it'd be more gaudy?" Blair asks, dropping her bag onto the small couch. A small tray of drinks sits on the sleek, black coffee table in front of her.

"Want me to request a few ancient statues? Would that make it better?"

Blair laughs. "I guess you'll just have to take me to the museums to see them then."

Finding the door to the bedroom, I swing it open. It's just as extravagant as the rest of the suite. The doors are open to the balcony that hides the city views with a wall of plants and flowers, no doubt for privacy. The king bed—sitting on a raised platform—is covered in pillows of all sizes.

Blair's eyes look like they are going to pop out of her head they are so big.

"You okay with this?"

"I just…"

"Just what?"

Blair's mouth opens and closes, not quite finding the right words. "I didn't expect us to have to share a bed."

"It's not the end of the world."

"At least it's a king?"

It comes out more of a question.

"I can sleep on the couch if it makes you more comfortable."

"No." She's quick to answer. "For three weeks? It's fine. Fine."

"Right." I nod. "Fine."

Except it's anything but fine. Watching Blair move around the room—the graceful way she moves—sends dirty thoughts racing through my mind. I want to throw her down on the bed and taste her lips. Peel her out of that outfit of hers. Do what I've wanted to do since I met her at the airport.

"I'm pretty sure my entire apartment can fit into this bathroom."

Blair's head pops out from the bathroom. I move to where she is, taking in yet another over-the-top space.

An ornate clawfoot tub.

Dual vanity with makeup station.

Glass shower with at least three showerheads that I can see.

It's the epitome of luxury.

"I wouldn't mind taking a dip in that bath."

Her heated gaze meets mine. Is she having the same thoughts as me? Feeling this instant connection that I can't seem to get rid of?

I have one goal in mind.

To get traveLLin'. It's all I want.

And I'm not going to let Blair and those inquisitive eyes of hers distract.

At least more than she already is.

"We need to get downstairs for the welcome cocktails."

Blair's voice cuts through my thoughts—thoughts that I need to force down. Deep down, because the last thing I need is to get attached to someone whose presence in my life is temporary.

As long as I keep reminding myself of that the next few weeks, I'll be fine.

Maybe.

I hope.

Blair tucks a stray piece of hair behind her ear. I follow the movement, watching as her fingers brush against the pulse in her neck.

Damn it.

This is going to be the furthest thing from fine.

Chapter Seven

BLAIR

Deep breaths, Blair. You can do this.

With our plane getting in later than originally anticipated, we had just enough time to drop our bags off in the room before hurrying down to the welcome hour.

I wish I had more time to freshen up. To try and get my legs under me. From the minute I shook hands with her, my mind has been a swirly mess.

"You coming, tartlet?"

Raven's words stir me out of my spiral.

"Tartlet? Really?" I quirk a brow as I pass her on the way out of the elevator.

"It felt wrong the second it came out," she answers with a laugh.

The lobby restaurant is bustling with guests.

Old. Young.

People with bright turquoise mohawks. My own simple blonde hair.

Men. Women.

I had no idea this many people would turn out to try and nab this company.

"Are they all here for traveLLin'?"

Raven nods, grabbing a cocktail from the bar.

"Cocktail?"

I nod, taking the proffered orange-colored drink. The bubbles help cool my overwhelming nerves.

"Why is no one talking to each other?" I cover my whisper with the glass.

Raven's eyes take in the room as we find an empty spot at a high-top table.

"I don't think I've done something this awkward since my first time."

"I'm sorry?" I almost spit my drink out. God, what a first impression that would make on these people.

"I'm serious." Raven looks around.

"You'd think this many people from different walks of life would have more in common, but they don't."

Now that she mentions it, everyone is clinging to the walls like they're needed to hold it up. A few people are mingling, but no one is making the first move.

"Do you think they just don't want to be the first person to break the ice?"

"One would think they'd try since it's what's required of them for this job."

"Oh yeah?" I cross my arms, leaning across the table. "What exactly is required for this job?"

"Not this." Raven waves a hand around the crowd. "If I were the one that had to break this down for a feature, I'd say don't come here because drying paint is more interesting than these people."

An unladylike snort leaves me, choking over the fizz in my drink. "I can safely say you're more interesting than that."

"And even if I wasn't, fake it 'til you make it, right?"

"Easier said than done," I whisper over my glass.

"We've got this," Raven tells me, her voice quiet. "Act like you've seen me naked and you'll be fine."

Heat blooms in my cheeks.

That's the last thing I need to be doing.

"Relax. We'll be fine. No one will know about us."

"Know what?"

I jump at the voice behind us.

Turning, I see an older woman with reddish brown hair and a studying look on her face.

"That this is our first time in Milan." Raven links her arm with mine. "Raven West. And you must be Laney."

Oh shit. Eden's wife. No doubt Raven did her homework on both of them.

Crap. Did she hear any of our conversation?

"Wonderful to meet you, Raven. And you are?" She holds her hand out to me.

"Blair Stevens."

"Lovely to meet you both. First time in Milan, then?" She sips on her drink. "You must be excited."

"I can't wait," I tell her. "I want to pack as much as I can in these next few weeks."

"If you need any travel tips, you know where to find us."

"Good evening, everyone." A loud voice crackles over the speakers. Raven straightens, turning to find an older woman with short gray hair, dressed in a fashionable tunic, with a mic by the bar. "I'm Eden Sands and welcome to Milan!"

"That's my cue, ladies." She waves us off and goes to find her wife.

This gets the first reaction out of people all night.

"My wife, Laney, and I are so happy you all could join us these next few weeks. I know this is a bit unusual, but seeing as how the company is travel-based, I figured what better way to get to know people than on a trip."

A few enthusiastic people cheer her on. Raven is watching her with rapt attention, brown eyes so focused that an asteroid could slam into the earth and she wouldn't notice.

"We've curated some of our favorite places in Milan to take you to over the next few weeks. We hope you have the time of your lives, and I can't wait to get to know you."

Turning the mic off, people swarm her as she makes her way through the crowd.

"Eden, come meet Raven and Blair." Laney guides her over to the two of us.

Patting down her hair, Raven gives me a nervous smile.

Mingling and making small talk with people? This is something that comes naturally to me working in the prosecutor's office.

"Wonderful to meet you," we both tell her, shaking her hand.

"It's their first time here," Laney informs her wife.

"Brilliant!" Eden's face lights up. "I know you two will just adore it."

"I've always wanted to come here, and I'm so happy that Raven and I can do it together."

Eden drops a kiss on Laney's cheek. "Italy is better with your love, isn't that right?"

They share a warm look. One that tells me they've been happily in love for years. Something I wish I had. Or, that I wasn't only pretending to have right at this moment.

"I hope we get to see as much as possible while we're here."

"Eden is going to keep you two so busy, you won't have time to put your feet up," Laney laughs.

"Maybe if we're in that tub of ours," Raven tells them. "I wouldn't mind a nice relaxing day here."

"Then you'll love the spas here," Eden says. "To die for. Really, everything is in Milan. That's why I picked here."

"I'm not complaining at all," I confirm. Because if this is the first bit of Milan that I've seen, it won't be a hardship to be here for a few weeks.

"You two must be exhausted. We'll let you get going and see you soon?" Eden waves us goodbye before meeting with the others around us.

Raven sways, betraying just how tired she really is.

"C'mon." Giving her hand a tug, I pull her toward the elevators. "We can mingle more tomorrow."

"That went well, right?" Raven asks as we head back to our suite.

"I think it did."

As tired as Raven is, I'm wide awake at the thought of sharing a bed with her.

Raven slides the key over the lock and pushes open the door.

Neither one of us is overly chatty as we get ready for bed.

As I'm in the bathroom brushing my teeth, my mind keeps going back to having to sleep with the bombshell in the next room.

I give myself a pep talk as I slide into my satin tank and sleep shorts—pajamas I thought no one else would be seeing.

Shutting off the lights in the bathroom, I find Raven sitting in bed, wearing an oversized T-shirt. She shouldn't look as enticing as she does.

Raven rolls her eyes when she sees me hesitate, sliding her eye mask down into place. "I don't bite."

Except what if I want her to?

Jesus, get it together, Blair.

Sliding under the duvet next to her, I'm as still as possible. Just the proximity to Raven is messing with my head.

The smell of her perfume.

The heat coming from her body.

And now having to share a bed with her?

Night one and being around Raven is tempting. Too tempting for my liking.

I don't know how I'm going to survive the next few weeks with her.

Raven West may be the end of me.

But what a way to go.

Chapter Eight

"Are you ready for today?" I tap away on my phone, sending yet another email for an acquisition that needs my attention.

Even in Italy, I can't escape work. Being the CEO means no rest. I have to be accessible at all times.

Most days, I don't mind it.

But being in Milan with Blair?

I wouldn't mind having more than one minute alone with her.

From the moment we arrived at the airport in Seattle, it seems like we've been going a thousand miles per hour.

After checking in, there was a cocktail hour with everyone interested in buying the company, then we had a free day to rest and tour the city. I kept getting distracted by work while the two of us went out to explore.

So far, everything about Blair is impressing people. I could tell Laney and Eden both liked her. No doubt she could charm the pants off any person.

I wish I could hate the fact that we have to share a bed,

but I don't. I hate that I can't pull her into my arms and taste her. I want to wake up tangled around her.

Being that close to her is going to be the biggest distraction these next few weeks.

"Duomo Tour, right?"

Movement from the bedroom catches my eye as Blair walks into the living room. Setting my phone down on the bar, I drink in the woman in front of me.

Sweeping blonde hair curls around her shoulders. A simple, white T-shirt that hugs her curves is tucked into a pair of dark jeans with white tennis shoes to round out the look. My eyes snap back up to hers to find them raking over me.

I shift under her steady gaze. The thrum of my pulse picks up, echoing in my ears. It's not supposed to be like this.

I'm not supposed to *feel* anything for Blair Stevens. She was brought here to make me look like a well-rounded person. Someone whose life is more than work.

Even though I was firing off emails for the last twenty minutes.

But that's beside the point.

When Blair's eyes connect with mine, a flush colors her cheeks. I wonder what else of hers turns that color.

"Raven?"

"Sorry, what?"

I shake my head clear of any thoughts that would take me down the wrong road. This is a transaction. Plain and simple.

No need to get feelings or any other body parts involved.

"We're going to the Duomo?"

I nod, swallowing down the last of my orange juice sitting next to my phone. "Have you ever been?" God, I could smack myself for being so stupid. "Right, never been to Italy before, so of course not."

What is it about Blair that turns me into a bumbling buffoon? I can stare down CEOs of any company without breaking a sweat. Yet, the woman who is pretending to be my girlfriend is the one twisting up my insides?

Get it together, Raven.

"Duomo then lunch on our own."

Blair leans across me, grabbing a grape and popping it into her mouth. The citrusy scent that follows her overwhelms me.

"Ready to go then?"

"Yes."

And ready to breathe some Blair-free air.

THE TOUR GUIDE GOES ON. And on. And on.

The history of the building we're in. How it came to be. It helps distract me from where we are— on the roof of this impressive church.

Being outside in the midst of it is stunning. Even something I can appreciate as I stay in the middle of the roof.

I hate heights. And seeing how high up we are right now? I wish I could take the express elevator down to the ground floor.

The Duomo, though, is best seen like this—experiencing the true beauty rather than hearing about it secondhand.

Except Blair is eating up every word. She's been asking questions the entire time, and I can't help but wish she was asking me these kinds of questions.

There's something about her. I want to learn everything about her. She's complicated. I want her to let me in.

It drives me crazy. I'm the kind of person that has people opening up to me within minutes. Sharing their life story.

So why can't I get Blair to?

Her steps are guarded as she walks over to me. People surround us everywhere on the roof.

"Have you ever seen something so beautiful?" Blair steps up to my elbow. Dark sunglasses hide her eyes, but her head is on a swivel, turning every which way to take it all in.

"I haven't."

She turns to face me, a small smile playing on her lips. "Have you even looked at the view?"

She's the only view I want—no, need—right this very minute.

"How can you not? No wonder Eden settled in Milan. It's incredible."

The Duomo looms large over the square, its fingers casting long shadows in its wake. Ornate, gothic architecture is a visual feast. With the pillars reaching into the sky, it's like we're in our own town up here.

"I wish we had more time here." Her voice is wistful, carried away on the wind, like she doesn't want anyone to know she won't be able to come back.

"Hey." I hook my hand around her elbow and pull her into me. "It just means we'll make the most of all the time we have here."

That earns me a real smile. "I plan on it. Even if I have to drag you along."

"Hey! Who said you'd have to drag me anywhere?"

Blair shrugs a shoulder, pushing her sunglasses up onto

her head. "You didn't seem that interested in hearing about the history of this place."

"Because I'm trying to focus on not falling over the edge," I mutter.

Blair goes to peek down over the ledge, but I pull her back.

"Don't get too close!"

Blair laughs, deep and bright and full. "You realize there's an entire other level down there, right?"

I step closer to the edge, giving it a safe distance to see more people below us.

"It's like this place keeps on going."

"C'mon." Blair links her hand with mine and pulls me off with her.

My breath hitches in my throat as I follow her down the narrow steps.

It has nothing to do with the way she's holding my hand. Or the way it sends frissons of heat through me, my heart beating double time in my chest.

"The view is even better down here."

Blair leans against the railing, looking down over the tiny people in the square. Groups of tourists are taking photos, others mingling in sidewalk cafés.

With the blue skies, it's postcard worthy.

I try not to step too close to the edge.

"Are you scared of heights?" Blair turns, curious eyes meeting mine when I stay back from her.

"I wouldn't say scared. More like giving them the respect they deserve from a safe distance."

Blair smirks, leaning back against the side of a pillar. "And here I didn't think you were scared of anything."

"I didn't say scared."

"Then come here." She holds her hand out to me, and I take it without thought.

"You're not scared of heights?" I whisper, trying not to focus on how small everyone looks below us.

"I'm not scared of much these days."

Blair scoots me closer to the edge, and my grip on her tightens. Digging my nails into her arms, I don't let go.

"I promise," Blair whispers, close to my ear, "I won't let anything happen to you."

It's those words that have me relaxing into her hold.

How can a woman I've only known for a short while have such power over me?

I don't want to give it to her, but she's taken it.

Right here on the roof of this imposing structure in Milan.

It was the thing I wasn't expecting to happen. But somehow, Blair has crawled under the defenses I use to keep the world at bay and is slotting herself into my life.

I'd stay up here with her for ages if it meant I got to keep her.

Heights be damned.

Chapter Nine

BLAIR

"Have you ever been to a place like this?" Raven asks. She shucks out of her coat and hangs it in one of the small wooden stalls.

"Can't say that I have."

Everything here is older than our entire country. The thermal spa that Eden rented for our group today is outside of the city. The locker room is made up of old brick walls and low hanging lights, accompanied by wooden stalls. Candles and bouquets of fresh flowers sit on the counters, perfuming the air.

"You'll enjoy it," Raven tells me. "A good way to relax."

Raven winks at me before starting to change into her suit. I turn around, not wanting her to catch me staring.

I have no idea how this is going to be relaxing for me when the entire time I've been in Milan, I've been strung like a live wire ready to snap.

Every time I'm around Raven, my thoughts fill up with all the dirty things I want to do to her. How I want to see her spread out before me—naked.

"Ready?" Her voice pulls me out of my wandering thoughts.

"Yes." I give her a small smile, tying the fuzzy robe they gave us around me.

I follow Raven without question. A few people are already getting couples' massages, but that's where I drew the line. A spa is one thing. Knowing someone is rubbing Raven down just feet away from me?

I don't think I could take it.

Pushing open the door to the spa, I'm shocked when I see it's outside. Because it's late, the sun is starting to set, giving it an ethereal glow.

The grass is spongy beneath my sandals. Only a few people are out here. I'm starting to recognize some of them, but most have stayed to themselves.

Archways are cut into the old brick walls. They are lit up from the inside, casting a low glow across the spa. The sounds of the city are distant from here.

Raven slips out of her robe, and my jaw hits the ground.

The black one-piece clings to her every curve. A V dips low between her breasts, drawing my eyes to her chest. But the real highlight? The high cut bottom shows off her tantalizing legs. With her long dark hair swept over one shoulder, she looks like a goddess.

One I wouldn't mind worshipping.

"You ready?" Raven's warm hand comes down on my forearm, eliciting a gasp.

"Sorry, yes."

I strip out of my robe into my own basic swimsuit. It's nothing fancy, a simple two-piece in red that I've had for years.

Still, I don't miss the way Raven's eyes travel over me as I step into the warm water.

"Ohhh."

"Good?" Raven slips in beside me.

"I could live here."

Raven laughs, swimming to one of the built-in chairs in the large pool. "I wouldn't mind it."

"Yeah?" I swim toward another one, lying down and taking in the quickly setting sun.

"Having access to a place like this? It might get me out of the office every now and then."

I wish I could do something like this more often. But with the stress of real life, it's nice to play pretend. Because right now, it's easy to picture this being my life. Not a care in the world. Not stressing about work or money or Avi.

Just…enjoying myself. Because I can.

If only it didn't make me feel selfish.

"Stop it."

"Huh?" I glance over at Raven. Her head is turned toward me, resting on the tiled chair.

A smile quirks her beautiful mouth. "I can hear you thinking from here."

"Sorry."

"Don't be. Anything you need to get off your chest?"

I sigh. It'd be so easy to confide in Raven. To get swept up in the notion that she actually is my girlfriend. But do I really need to unload my problems onto her?

"Just trying to relax."

"Here." Raven slides over onto my seat, putting herself between me and the back of the chair. Her hands dig into my shoulders.

"Oh God."

The moan that slips out is indecent.

"Is this okay?"

I nod because it's more than okay. Having Raven's

hands on me like this, digging into the tired muscles, feels good.

Too good.

I want to feel her hands everywhere.

"You're really tight."

Raven's thumbs trail over the muscles in my neck. Her touch is tender as I relax into it. She doesn't say anything, just continues to work on the knots.

I dig my fists into my thighs, needing to control myself. Because what I really want to do?

I want to spin in this chair and kiss the life out of Raven.

The vixen is consuming my every thought. I don't know how this woman is still single. She is the most captivating person I have ever met in my entire life.

In only a few short days, I've fallen under her spell.

With every pass of Raven's hands over me, the tension I've been carrying around starts to release. I become more relaxed, feeling like a noodle.

"Better?" Raven whispers against my ear.

A shudder travels my body. Again, I can only nod because words fail me.

Every single part of me is wrapped up in this woman. It shouldn't be like this. We've barely been here two weeks, and I'm crushing on the woman who is my girlfriend.

My *fake* girlfriend. I have no time in my life for a woman like Raven. Someone like her deserves to be showered with everything they could ever want.

Time. Affection. Love.

If only that person could be me.

But it's not.

Raven West will be my undoing.

Chapter Ten

BLAIR

"Mmm. That feels so good."

Raven's hair is just as soft as it looks. Even softer as I fist it, holding her face to my pussy. Her tongue is magic as it flutters across my clit.

"Just wait."

A finger slips inside, touching that hidden spot so few women have been able to find. It shouldn't be a surprise that Raven can.

The woman can do no wrong.

Each curl is pushing me closer and closer to flying off the edge.

"I'm so close, Raven."

"Come for me, Blair."

Blair.

Just my name vibrating from her lips has me right on the cusp of an orgasm. I'm squeezing her tight to me, riding her face. It's so close, I can feel the edges of my vision darkening.

"Holy shit."

"Blair?"

My voice sounds far away. The lusty spell Raven put me under fades.

"Blair?" This time, her voice is clear.

"Holy shit."

My eyes fly open. The bed next to me is empty.

Holy shit.

I just had a sex dream about Raven.

Raven, who is now walking into the room looking every bit as sexy as she has for the past week.

Wearing a black maxi skirt, a high slit exposes her graceful legs. A chambray shirt is open to the swells of her breasts.

I sit up, pulling the duvet up to my neck.

The satin camisole I sleep in won't hide how hard my nipples are.

For Raven.

I can't believe I had a sex dream about the woman who is paying me to be here. Money that is desperately needed.

Damn that massage she gave me at the spa yesterday.

"Morning." I do my best to control my voice and not sound like some sex-addled maniac.

"I didn't want to wake you, but there's been a change of plans for today."

"Oh yeah?"

She nods, her brow furrowing in confusion. I can't imagine how I look right now.

"We'll be visiting a winery, so we need to be ready to leave in an hour."

"No problem." I give her what I hope is a reassuring smile.

"Are you okay?"

I rake a hand through my hair, getting stuck in the knots. Apparently the dream was even better than I thought because everything about me is a mess.

"I'm good. Just need to get cleaned up."

Raven doesn't look convinced. "I have a few emails to answer. I'll be in the living room when you're ready to leave."

"Perfect." I give her a thumbs-up.

She spins on her heel and leaves. Once the door clicks shut behind her, I collapse back onto the pile of pillows.

A thumbs-up? *Really, Blair?*

Raven is turning me into a teenager who has the hots on her model crush. Every inch of my body is still alight with lust.

I know I shouldn't do it—not when Raven is in the next room—but I can't help myself.

Brushing my fingers under the band of my underwear, I'm wet. And sensitive.

Holy shit.

Everything about that dream felt real. Raven's hair in my hand. Her deep, chocolate eyes staring up at me as she worked me over.

Now that I've touched my clit, I'm so close to coming, I need to get off. That dream was a tease. I wish it were her fingers strumming over my clit and not mine.

I'm still picturing the woman with her face buried between my legs. Each stroke of my finger pushes me closer to the edge.

The thought of my hands tangled in her silky soft hair as she tongues me has me tipping over the edge.

I come on a quiet cry. It's harder than I've come in a while. All at my own hand. Because of the woman who brought me halfway across the world to impress some old lesbian.

Everything is swirling together in my head. This should not be happening. I should not be getting off to thoughts of Raven, let alone having sex dreams about her.

What is wrong with me?

Throwing back the fluffy, white duvet, I pad into the bathroom. My nipples are diamond hard in the mirror under my silk camisole. My face is flushed and my hair is a mess from sleep.

I look thoroughly fucked. Dropping my underwear and pulling off my top, I start the shower. If I have any hope of making it through the day with Raven, I need to get my desire for her under control.

Steam fills the bathroom. It does nothing to help temper the heat still coursing through me. I throw the handle toward cold and take the fastest shower on record.

A knock sounds at the door as I'm toweling off.

"Can I..." Raven peeks through the door. Her dark eyes find mine in the mirror. There's a flush to her cheeks. Even though I'm hidden behind the tempered glass, it's like I can feel her eyes roam over every inch of bare skin.

What I wouldn't give to feel her hands on me that way.

"Sorry. I just need to grab a few things to finish getting ready."

"Sure."

I tug the towel tighter around me. I don't need to give Raven a peep show of any kind. She grabs what she needs and darts out of the bathroom.

Fuck.

Today is going to be a long day if I can't get my feelings for her under control.

Chapter Eleven

RAVEN

"Where are we going today?" Blair asks from her seat next to me on the bus. For the first time today, she's looking at me and not avoiding eye contact.

When she was finally ready, she looked gorgeous in black jeans, a white tee, and a faux leather jacket. If I had a motorcycle, I'd want to throw her on the back and take her for a ride.

God, I can't remember the last time I've acted so lusty.

We rattle down a quiet country road. It's a postcard-picture of the Italian countryside. Rolling hills. Green trees as far as the eye can see. A villa here and there.

I can't help but take in the gorgeous landscape with bright blue skies as we drive by. Even more so because Blair is so captivated by it.

"A little place I know."

"Of course you know a little place."

"Hey. I've never actually been here."

"Then how do you know about it?"

I smile. "My grandparents."

The bus slows and pulls down another tree-lined street.

A terra-cotta-colored building comes into view. Smaller buildings are in the distance, breaking up the perfectly lined rows of trees. An older man and his wife are waiting for us as we all unload.

"Ciao! Ciao!"

His thick Italian voice shouts at us, beckoning us to him.

"Ciao!" Eden returns his greeting with gusto. "I can't thank you enough for fitting us in today, Marco."

He waves her off. "I'm glad you are here. Less wine for me," he guffaws, patting a wide belly.

"And a special thank you to Raven for connecting us with Marco." Eden's eyes find mine in the crowd.

"I'm happy to help."

"Then let's drink wine!" Marco claps his hands, leading us into the old building.

"I can't believe you did all this." Blair sounds surprised. "Where do you find all the time?"

"I ran into Eden in the lobby, and the other one fell through today because of an issue with the vats. I knew about this place, so I suggested it. No big deal." I shrug a shoulder. "I had time this morning."

Blair's eyes widen.

"You okay?"

"Totally fine." Her voice goes up an octave before she grabs my arm. "Raven. This is big. Eden looks fucking ecstatic."

I'm trying not to let that small fact slip into my brain.

Of course I knew how happy she was when I told her I could make this work when I ran into her in the lobby this morning.

The tasting room is everything I remember seeing in pictures.

Wine bottles line one wall. Candles with wax dripping

over the edges of bottles sit on each table. Hardwood floors creak beneath our feet. Lines of glasses sit on each table as Marco's wife directs us each to a seat.

"Ladies, can I join you?" Eden asks as we find a spot near the window.

"Of course. It'd be our pleasure."

Blair pulls me down next to her, dropping an innocent peck on my cheek. "You've got this."

Her whisper is only for me.

"How are you ladies enjoying Milan so far?" Eden asks, green eyes flitting between the two of us.

"I love it," Blair answers. "I can't get over how incredible the Duomo tour was."

"It's one of my favorite places in the world."

Blair sips her wine. "I can see why. Stunning architecture."

"Did you enjoy it, Raven?" Eden asks, leaning her elbows on the table.

"I'd prefer to see it from the ground." I laugh.

"Ahh, you're like my Laney. She hates heights too."

"She and I would get along well then. Is she here with you today?"

Eden shakes her head. "She had to stay back and get some packing done. We're selling everything here and wandering."

"Wow. Where are you going first?" Blair asks.

"Going to spend some time in Budapest before following summer. No need to be cold if we don't have to."

"I'm trying to get Raven to take me somewhere warm after this, but real life beckons at home."

"Make sure she does." Eden points at me. "There's always going to be something at home. Make time for travel. And each other."

"I always do." I face Blair, tucking a loose strand of hair behind her ear. "Who wouldn't with this woman?"

Eden studies both of us with a careful eye. "How did you two meet?"

"We met at a work function," I answer before Blair can stutter her way through a response.

If there's one thing I've learned about Blair it's that lying doesn't exactly come easy to her. While it's something I would normally be grateful for, it's not under these circumstances.

"Was it love at first sight?"

"It took awhile for her to win me over," Blair laughs.

"And here I thought I was the most charming woman you'd ever met," I say in jest.

"So you think."

Eden's eyes are moving between the two of us. It sends an uneasy feeling through me. Every time we've been around her, we've been nothing but the picture-perfect couple, but her perusal still makes me tense.

"You two are lucky. Enjoy each other while you can." Eden finishes her glass and stands. "I'm going to go mingle with some of the other guests and let you enjoy your day. It was lovely getting to chat more with both of you."

"Wow." Blair turns wide eyes to me. "That couldn't have gone better."

I don't think. I wrap an arm around her shoulders and pull her into a hug. All the nerves fluttering inside calm at her touch.

Being around Eden makes me nervous. I want this company so bad, I don't know what I'll do if I don't get it. But Blair helps calm those nerves. Which is saying something since I've never been this desperate to get anything in my life.

"Thank you," I whisper.

"She's eating out of the palm of your hand, Raven."

"God, I hope so."

Blair pulls back, her cheeks pink. I love seeing her emotions play out on her face. She gulps down another sip of wine.

"How do you know about this winery?" she asks.

The sun is weak in the sky, hiding behind the clouds. This time of year, all of the trees are barren. It's oddly comforting.

"My grandparents visited. They went on a tour with other seniors and loved it here."

"And they liked it so much you wanted to come?"

"I wanted to see if it was worth all the fuss."

"And is it?"

I nod. "It's one of the reasons I want to buy traveLLin'. This winery? I know we're welcome because the tour that brought my grandparents here? She runs it with her girlfriend. This is a place I know people like us are welcome. I know what it's like to not feel that. And I never want people to encounter that."

"You're pretty incredible, you know that?"

"I'm not." I try to brush her off, but she won't let me.

"Yes you are. Most people would want to buy this just to have another company to add to their roster. But you love it."

I rest my hand in my chin, taking in this beautiful woman that I never would've met had it not been for traveLLin'.

I thought it would be hard to spend time with someone for the next few weeks. The only hard part about it is convincing myself not to fall for Blair.

Because the more time I spend in her company, the harder it is to keep my distance.

"Everything okay?" Raven asks.

It was a good day at the winery with her.

No.

A *great* day.

I find that the more time I spend with her, the less this thing starts to feel fake between us.

Raven can put anyone at ease. We've met a few of the other couples that are here to try and buy the company. They are fine. Nothing that would make me want to give my company over to them.

Maybe I'm biased, but Raven should be a lock to get it. No one else has the personality that she does to run this company. Or maybe it's the passion. Either way, she's perfect for it.

But it doesn't make it any easier to be away from my sister.

This was why I struggled with leaving. As much as this would help our living situation, it's hard to leave Avi. With so much upheaval in her life already, the last thing I want to do is feel like I'm leaving her behind.

I read the email from Avi again. Another issue with one of her teachers over some petty reason. It seems no matter what she does, they are going to have an issue with her. I don't know if it's because she doesn't come from a traditional family, but I do everything I can to make school easier for her.

A fruitless effort it seems.

"Sorry. Just missing home right now."

"Anything I can do to help?"

Raven drops onto the couch in our living room next to me. It's funny how over the course of our time here, this hotel suite has started to feel like a home away from home.

"Not really."

Raven's gaze is assessing, trying to figure out what could be the cause of my change in mood tonight. Because who could possibly be upset after spending the day in the Italian countryside drinking wine?

I'm not ready to tell her about Avi. She's the most important person in my life, and not something I use to gain sympathy.

"Want to get out of here?"

"And go where?" Darkness has settled upon Milan. We didn't get back until late, tipsy on wine and full of the finest foods Italy has to offer.

"I have an idea. Give me a few minutes."

Patting my knee, Raven taps on her phone before putting it to her ear. She paces in front of the terrace. Lights from the city filter in. With the soft glow of the lamps in the hotel room, she looks like an angel.

One that has been sent to whisk me away from my real life.

No matter how brief of a time.

"Let's go." She ends the call and holds out her hand to me.

"Go where?"

Her laugh is soft and sweet. "I promise, you'll love it."

I can't help but eye her suspiciously. When your younger sister comes and lives with you, you can't help but be wary of situations where you don't know what's coming.

I wish I weren't, but it's hard not to be.

"Okay."

Raven gives me a beaming smile as I take her hand. We exchange few words as we head down to the lobby and get into a waiting car.

Even though it's dark, I can see that people on the streets are dressed for the clubs.

"You better not be taking me to a club."

Raven rolls her eyes, turning to face me in the backseat of the car. "Blair, please. I know you by now."

"And?" I question.

"And the last thing you'd want to do is go to a club."

"You're right. So where are we going?" I cross my eyes, letting my knees bump with hers in the back of the car.

"We're here."

The car slows to a stop as Raven points to an older building in a quiet square. A small café has a few patrons under sidewalk umbrellas, but other than that, it's empty. We're away from the main tourist attractions here.

"What exactly is here?"

Raven ignores me as she grabs my hand—sending shockwaves through me—and leads me to a small side door of a brick building. After she exchanges a few words with the guard there, he smiles and then leads us inside.

"Raven…"

"Just wait," she shushes me.

Her smile is lighting up her entire face as the security guard opens another door and points us down a hallway.

"C'mon."

Raven tugs me after her in what gives way to a cavernous space. That opens up to Da Vinci's *The Last Supper*.

"Raven."

The painting takes up the entire wall before us. Dropping her hand, I get as close as I can. I don't think I've ever seen something so beautiful in my life.

People come from all corners of the globe to see this painting, and somehow, it's just the two of us.

The room is empty. Not a single person is in here. It's so quiet, you can hear a pin drop.

"It's stunning," I whisper.

The air feels different in here, like if I breathe too loudly, it'll upset the painting. I want to give it the respect it's due.

Without hordes of people, we get an up close and personal view of the piece.

The brush strokes.

The details of each person.

The imperfections.

"I've never seen anything so beautiful."

"Me neither."

I turn to face Raven, but her eyes are on me. The way her eyes are seeing me—truly seeing me—has my heart stuttering in my chest.

It shouldn't be like this. Not with someone who isn't my girlfriend. Not my real girlfriend anyway.

"How'd you know I would want to see this?"

She only shrugs a shoulder. "I thought it might be on your list."

Closing the distance between us, I wrap her in a hug. Being with her here calms every anxious nerve I was feeling earlier. Which is no easy feat.

Raising Avi on my own basically guarantees I'm on

edge all the time.

Except now. Right now, all I have to think about is Raven and the gift of peace she's given me in the form of a painting that's hundreds of years old.

"Thank you."

"You don't have to thank me." Her breath ghosts over my neck, sending shivers through me. God, every move this woman makes has me yearning for her that much more.

"How did you make this happen?" My voice is in awe as I absorb every detail of the painting.

"With a large enough donation, anything can happen."

Raven continues to surprise me. "No one has ever done anything like this for me before."

"You deserve to see everything you want to on this trip."

I want to kiss her. To shower her with the passion she deserves from a woman. Because as much as Raven has said her work is her life, she deserves someone that would put her first.

I wish it could be me. I wish I could give Raven every part of me, except I can't. God, I wish I could.

Most people wouldn't go to so much trouble to see some old historic painting. But Raven did.

Within a few days, she's learned what I like and dislike. And nothing could take my mind off missing my sister like this.

Pulling back, I stare into the deep brown depths of her eyes. There is nothing but sincerity there, wanting to make my own pain go away.

"Seriously, thank you for this."

"Again, no thanks needed."

Our voices echo in the quiet of the hall.

I shrug a shoulder, staring at the painting in front of

me. "I never would have gotten to see this in person if it weren't for you."

Raven's eyes are fierce as she holds my stare. "I would give you the world if I could."

And for a moment, I believe her.

Because Raven would be able to make that happen.

If only it were a world I existed in.

Chapter Thirteen

BLAIR

"Eden loves her cocktail hours."

The hotel is thrumming with people. Eden rented out the entire rooftop terrace tonight for another cocktail hour. I've started to recognize some of the people here, but mostly, everyone has kept to themselves, even after being here for a week.

"Are you saying you don't like free drinks overlooking Milan?" Raven asks. Her hand is linked with mine as we stand on the edges of the crowd.

From the moment her hand grabbed hold of mine tonight, I've been on edge. Every nerve in my body is clamoring to feel her touch.

After sharing such an intimate night with her at the church with Da Vinci's painting, things shifted between us. No matter how many times I keep telling myself this is all fake, my body isn't getting the memo.

I take a dramatic suck of my drink—a Campari Spritz—and turn my eyes to Raven. The lights reflect back to me. "I will never turn down one of these."

"Or a night with you."

Heat blazes in Raven's eyes. Even out here in the dark, it's apparent.

"Raven—"

"Can I interest either of you in pesto raviolis?" The waiter interrupts our conversation.

"Thank you." Raven grabs one, popping it into her mouth. "Oh my God. You have to try that."

She moans around a mouthful.

Does she not realize she's driving me crazy?

The sounds coming from her are sinful. Pair those with the simple black dress she's wearing, and I'm ready to jump into the pool to douse the inferno ripping through me.

"That's good," I agree, trying to temper my body.

"C'mon, let's go mingle some more."

I trail after Raven, watching as she works the crowd. She's a natural. I can see why she's the CEO of her own company. Everyone is enthralled with her. Wanting more.

The same as me.

The more time I spend with her, the more I want to be around her.

"Sorry."

Someone bumps into me from behind. Instead of falling, I catch myself on Raven. Face to face, I feel her curves under my hands and the way her fingers tighten against my biceps. Her tongue peeks out to wet her bottom lip.

Fuck.

I'm done waiting.

If this short amount of time here is the only time I get with her, I want to make the most of it.

Grabbing her hand, I lead her toward the elevator and find a quiet spot away from the noise.

"Blair, what are you—"

Pushing her against the wall, I seal my mouth over

hers. I swallow her gasps as I push my tongue into her mouth.

She meets me stroke for stroke. Cool hands drift under my coat, pulling me closer. I thrust a leg between hers, deepening the kiss.

Every moan, every whimper I devour.

This kiss is everything I imagined it would be. I tear my lips from her mouth, trailing kisses along her jaw. Sucking at the soft skin of her neck.

"I want you." I tug her earlobe between my teeth.

"Blair," Raven whines, pulling my mouth back to hers. She flips us, pushing me against the wall. "Yes."

She slants her mouth over mine, trailing her hands lower, dipping into the waistband of my jeans. The heat coming off her is burning me alive.

"I'm tired of denying myself this."

Raven clutches my coat, holding me to her. Her lips are slick from my kisses.

Fuck, wanting her like this only makes me more wet.

I trail a finger up her arm. Goose bumps break out in its wake. She feels this too. Thank God, because if it were only me, I don't know what I'd do.

"Do you want to go back to the room?"

Her eyes are glassy as she bites down on her bottom lip. "Yes. Now."

The command in her voice is there. It's the Raven I've gotten to know in this short time.

But tonight? I'm taking it back from her.

Leading us to the elevators, I keep her at a distance. There's people coming and going, and the last thing she needs is to be found in a compromising position.

I don't want to do anything to jeopardize why we're here.

I keep my hands to myself as the elevator carries us to our floor.

Raven waves the keycard over the lock and pushes into the room.

"Stop." My voice echoes against the walls of the space.

Raven stands still in the middle of the room. The soft glow of the lights make her look otherworldly.

"Do you have any idea how much you've been driving me crazy?" I tell her, stepping up behind her.

The cool silk of her dress catches as I drag a finger down her side.

"I can say the same for you."

"You're always in control." I nip at her neck. "The CEO."

She nods.

"Not tonight." I lick a path up her neck. "Tonight, I hold all the power."

The snick of her zipper echoes in the large room as I pull it down. The fabric sags as I expose more of her skin. Each delicious inch has my mouth watering.

"I can't wait to have my way with you tonight." I press a kiss to her shoulder.

I push her dress off her shoulders, strip her of her bra and underwear and drink my fill of her bare body.

"You are fucking gorgeous."

I trace her curves with a fingertip. From her full, round ass, around her hip, and to her front.

Raven's eyes are dark and wide. Her skin is pebbled from the cool air of the hotel room. Her teeth dig into her bottom lip.

Yes.

This is exactly how I want her.

"Are you wet for me?"

She nods.

I lick a trail up the gentle slope of her neck to her ear, tugging the lobe between my teeth. "Use your words, Raven."

"Yes."

"Have you been like this all night?"

I drag my finger lower, hovering above her bare pussy. Teasing. Edging. Wanting to increase her pleasure.

"Mmm-hmm."

I slide my finger lower before reversing and trailing back up toward her beautiful breasts.

Her nipples are diamond hard.

"Do you want to come?"

"Yes." Her breath leaves her in a gasp.

Raven West is the sexiest woman I've ever laid eyes on. She's power and strength bottled up. One not to be messed with.

But right now? Right now, she's giving herself over to me.

And I can't wait to take everything from her.

Not yet.

Tonight, she's my plaything. And I want to have my way with her.

"Go to the bedroom. Lie down and spread those legs for me."

"Yes."

She spins on her red-soled heels. There's a sway to her hips that is absolutely captivating. I can't wait to sink my teeth into her tonight. To let her come on my tongue.

I'm aching—soaked—wanting to have her.

"Oh, and Raven?"

She stops, throwing a coy look over her shoulder.

"Keep the heels on."

Chapter Fourteen

RAVEN

My body is a live wire ready to snap. Buzzing anticipation courses through my veins as I wait for Blair to join me.

Lying on the bed, I spread myself out for her. The click of the door shutting draws my attention to the woman walking toward me.

No. Stalking toward me.

God, she is so sexy. It's been so hard to keep my hands off her.

I never thought I'd actually be attracted to my fake girl-friend. But Blair? Blair is something else entirely.

Every move she makes draws me further into her bubble. I shouldn't want to spend every second of my time here with her, but I do.

She's the first person in a long time to shift my focus from work. Even though that's the very reason we're here.

"Thinking some pretty deep thoughts there, Raven."

Even her voice—the way she says my name—has heat flowing through me.

Her gaze is assessing as she stops at the foot of the bed.

"Thinking about you."

"Oh yeah?" She steps closer, clasping her hand around my ankle. "What about?"

Her thumb strokes my ankle, sending me reeling. "How I'm ready for you to fuck me."

"Look at you." She drags a finger from my ankle to my knee and back. "All laid out for me and ready for me to do whatever I want with you."

I squirm under her touch. "Yes."

"Yes to which part?"

"All of it."

Blair shifts, resting a knee on the bed next to my hip. The slightest brush of her against me has heat gathering in my pussy.

"Arms up."

I immediately follow her demand.

"So good at following directions."

"If it gets your mouth on me…"

Blair bends over, her hair falling around us. Her eyes are hungry with lust. "Is that what you want?"

Her hand traces my hip bone, circling my belly button before settling just under my breasts.

I can't remember the last time I've been so worked up for a woman. I haven't been with someone like this in a long time. And here I am with Blair.

The woman who is driving me out of my mind.

"Blair."

"What do you need?"

"Everything."

"Hmm. Sounds like a tall order."

"One that you can hopefully help me with."

Her hand moves over my bare breast, giving it a squeeze that I feel everywhere.

"Yes!"

My shout isn't quiet.

"I love how responsive you are to me," Blair whispers at my ear before tugging my lobe between her teeth.

"It feels so good."

My nipple is hard as she tweaks it between her fingers. I arch into her touch. Needing it. Needing more. Needing everything she will give me.

Blair hovers over me, trailing warm kisses from my neck down between my breasts and over my stomach.

"I've imagined this," Blair confesses.

"You have?"

She licks a trail up my thigh. "Mmm, yes. Except you were eating me out."

"Maybe that'll be next time."

"Yes. Because right now, I'm going to devour you."

Her mouth closes around me and I arch into her touch. "Holy shit!" I thread my fingers through her hair, no longer caring about her demands to keep them over my head.

That tongue of hers is magic. Stroking, licking inside me. Driving me wild.

Nothing has ever felt as good as Blair Stevens's mouth on me.

"God, Blair. I'm so close."

"I want to feel you come on my tongue."

She continues her attack on my pussy, and the more she strums her tongue over my clit, the crazier she makes me.

When Blair curls her finger inside me, I explode.

"Fuck!" I scream. I don't care how loud I am. I give in to the pleasure flowing through me.

It's been so long since I've felt even remotely this good. It's like electricity has zapped my entire body.

"That's it, baby." Blair presses kisses against my thighs before I pull her up and over me.

"So good." I pull her mouth to mine, tasting my release on her lips. Our tongues tangle in a languid kiss.

I wedge my thigh between her legs and hold her close.

"Use me. Get off on me."

A lazy smile plays on her lips as she leans back, divesting herself of her clothes. When she's naked above me, I can't help but drink her in.

"Yes," she hisses, rubbing her clit against my leg. Her head is thrown back in pleasure as I lick a path over the pulse in her neck.

Seeing her like this is making me hot. Amping my pleasure up again.

"You feel so good," Blair whispers. "So fucking good."

"Are you going to come for me like a good girl?"

Her moves become frantic as she rubs against me. My hand slides between the two of us, cupping her breast in my hand. Its heavy weight is delicious as I continue my assault with my mouth. Every bit of bare skin calls to me.

A blush breaks out across Blair's chest as her shouts reach a fever pitch.

"Yes! Yes, Raven, yes! Yes, yes, yes!"

She comes undone in my arms and I hold her to me.

Blair collapses against me, our limbs in a tangle.

"Oh my God," she mutters against the side of my chest. "That was…"

"Yeah."

I know what she means without putting it into words. It seems like every cell in my body rearranged itself and will only answer to the woman who just made my world explode in an array of color.

"I plan on doing that again."

"You do?"

I twist a lock of soft hair between my fingers. "Several times in fact. I'm not stopping at one orgasm with you."

Blair props her chin on my chest, staring me in the eye. Eyes that are hazy after intense sex.

"Good. Because I plan on getting several more from you."

"Think we can skip tomorrow's events?"

Kissing her way up my chest, she hovers over me. "I fully support this. Now, get your ass into the shower. I want to clean you up before I have my way with you again."

I've never moved faster.

Chapter Fifteen

RAVEN

A bright burst of light pulls me from sleep. Every muscle in my body aches in the best way. It has a dopey smile spreading across my face.

I can't remember the last time I've had sex like that. If ever. I lost track of the number of orgasms Blair gave me.

With my job, I don't have the time for dating. Usually if I need something, I find what I want on a dating app. Nothing wrong with finding someone where we both need a mutual release.

Last night? That was the furthest thing from my mind. Last night was…wow. I never let myself go like that.

Who knew all of that dominance was packed inside Blair? Nothing has ever felt as good as being with her. Letting her take all the control. Giving myself over to her like that. I hope to make the most of my time with her here and do it again.

Maybe even a little something this morning to get the day started.

"Mmm, morning, Blair." Reaching across the bed, it's empty. The crumpled sheets are cool.

Dust floats through beams of sunlight that peek through the curtains. The bedroom is empty—no Blair in sight.

Going to the bathroom, I take care of business, brush my teeth, and grab a robe. Blair could not have gone far this morning, so I head to the living room.

It's there that I find her. Sitting on the couch in one of the thick hotel robes, she's typing away on her computer.

All that blonde hair of hers is pulled up into a messy bun. Fingers flying across the keyboard, her brows are pulled together in a tight look.

"Everything okay out here?"

She jumps, slamming the lid of her laptop closed.

"Sorry."

"Were you in the middle of something?"

She shakes her head. Tiny wisps of blonde hair escape her bun.

Fuck. Does she ever look stunning like this. No makeup. Face soft from last night.

"Just checking on things at home. A few emails here and there."

I drop down onto the coffee table in front of her. For once, work is the furthest thing from my mind.

TraveLLin'. West Investments. None of it matters as much as the woman sitting in front of me.

"And how is everything back home?"

"Good."

"Then does that mean I get you for the day?"

Blair's blue eyes rake over my body. The casual appraisal she gives me has butterflies swarming my belly.

What is it about Blair that ratchets up my desire like I've never known?

"Depends. What are we doing today?" She leans forward, hands resting on my knees.

I grab her elbows, pulling her close. Our knees knock together. Freckles line her face.

God, everything about her is exquisite. I want to gaze at every single part of her face and commit it to memory.

"How about dress shopping?"

"Dress shopping?" The corner of her mouth quirks up. "Are we getting married now?"

"Aren't you funny, but no. No title upgrades for you ye—"

Yet almost slips out on the end. I need to rein in my feelings for her. Keep them closer to the vest. No point in letting Blair know that I'm falling for her when this thing is going to be over soon enough.

"What do we need dresses for then?"

"The opera and the gala."

"The opera?" Blair questions. "We're going to the opera?"

"What, you don't want to hear Italians singing in a language you don't speak for three hours, waxing poetically about love and death?"

"Can't say that it's high on my list of things to do."

"Mine either, but at least we'll get to do it together."

"Suffering through the pain of Italians of the past."

I laugh. "What better way to spend the evening?"

Blair's eyes widen. "I can think of a few other things I'd like to do instead."

"Didn't get enough last night?"

"What can I say? I like making you come."

I groan, biting down on my bottom lip.

"How about I return the favor?"

"You did plenty of times last night, if I recall correctly."

"Mmm, yes." I place a warm kiss against her jaw. "But if I recall, I never got to taste you."

Dropping to my knees, I pull Blair to the edge of the sofa. Her legs fall open, baring herself to me.

She's already glistening. It's a heady sensation, knowing that I do this to Blair.

"Have you been like this all morning?" My hands coast up her thighs, moving the robe to the side.

"Since you woke up."

"Then it's only right I help you take care of this little problem."

The robe falls open, exposing her cleavage to me. I press light kisses to her chest. Licking and sucking on all the skin there. Savoring the taste of her under my tongue.

She squirms beneath me as my hands trace her hipbones.

"Raven," she whines. "Please."

"Please what?" I lick a trail up across her collarbone. Her pulse is throbbing in her neck. The blatant need coming off her is making me wet.

I'm ready to say fuck the plans for today and stay in bed with Blair. But I don't.

"Tell me what you want."

"I *need* you."

"You have me," I whisper against her.

In more ways than one.

I kiss my way back down her chest. Grabbing the tie of the robe with my teeth, I pull the knot loose.

Goose bumps cover her skin as I move my mouth lower.

Lower. Closer to where I want to be.

Using my elbows, I push her legs wider. The robe spills open. Her nipples are two hard peaks that I want to take between my teeth.

But not now.

Now, I want to taste this pussy of hers.

"Look how wet you are." I drag a finger through her folds. "I wonder how much it'll take to get you to come."

"Why don't you find out?" Blair whines.

"And not tease you the way you teased me last night?"

My finger goes higher, brushing against the soft patch of curls. I reverse the motion, taking care not to touch her clit. Not yet.

"Ugh." Her own hands start playing with her breasts. I want to bat them away, let her know that her orgasm is mine, but I don't care.

I love seeing how she takes care of her own pleasure.

But I'm not going to let this be a solo act.

Leaning over, I swipe my tongue through her pussy.

Fuck. She tastes so good. I don't know if I'll ever wipe the taste of her from my memory. Not that I'd want to.

"Gah!" She arches up into me, one hand forking through my hair to hold me in place.

The slight sting of pain opens the dam. I attack her pussy with a need I've never felt. I want every last drop Blair will give me.

I suck on her clit as I curl a finger inside her. Every moan of hers is driving me wild.

"Right there. So. Fucking. Good."

Blair is grinding down on my face. I can't get enough of her. She's squeezing the life out of my finger as I push a second one in.

"Are you going to come for me?" I pull back, sinking my teeth into the flesh of her thigh.

"I'm so close…so, so…"

I don't let her finish. I go back to sucking on her clit. Laving it with all my attention as I work my fingers in and out of her.

Electricity is swirling around us. One spark and the entire room could go up in flames.

But I couldn't care less. Not when Blair is this close to coming.

I curl my fingers inside her as I strum my tongue across her clit.

"Raven!"

She comes undone. Her head is thrown back in pleasure as I lap up every drop of her release.

"So good. So, so good," I praise her as the air settles back around us.

"I don't know if I have the energy to return the favor."

Blair is blissed out. Eyes closed, hair disheveled.

Fucking sexy as hell.

"This was about you." Pushing up, I drop a quick kiss on her lips. "You can have me later."

"Promise?" she asks, pulling me onto her lap.

"As long as you're not having any regrets about this."

"Only that we didn't do it sooner."

I give her a languid kiss, letting her taste herself on my lips. "And I plan on doing this every chance we get."

Because I don't want to waste a moment with Blair Stevens.

Chapter Sixteen

BLAIR

"Where exactly are we going shopping today?"

"Do you always have to know everything?" Raven smiles, pulling me closer to her on the crowded sidewalk.

With her heels on, she matches me in height. My smile mirrors hers. It's hard not to after the night we spent together.

And the morning.

"Yes. I don't like the unexpected."

My life has had too much unexpected. I like easy. I like predictable. Routine makes it all better for me.

"There's some shops just around the corner, and if you're lucky we can get gelato after."

"I already got lucky this morning. Gelato is happening."

"Good to know then." Raven drops a kiss on my cheek and draws to a stop in the middle of the sidewalk.

"Eden. Laney. Nice to see you."

Laney's gaze studies the two of us. The way her eyes flit back and forth has nerves coiling deep in my belly.

"Raven. Blair. What are you two up to today?"

Eden pulls off her sunglasses and tucks them into the front of her shirt. Her gray hair is stylishly coiffed into spikes. With a sweeping duster jacket on in a bright and colorful pattern, she looks every bit the fashionable Italian today.

"Doing a little shopping before the opera tonight." Raven links her arm with mine. "We've never been."

Eden's face goes wide with excitement. "It's fantastic. I know you'll have a wonderful time. Be sure to find us for a drink before the show tonight."

"Yes. We want to get to know more about you two as a couple." Laney's words are direct.

"That sounds great. We look forward to it," I tell her, swallowing down the nerves that rise up.

Eden seems to like us. Laney, on the other hand, I can't get a read on. Every time we're around her, I feel like she's going to figure out our secret and send us home. Like some business version of Survivor. That's the last thing I want to happen for Raven.

"Good, good. I don't want to keep you ladies. Enjoy your afternoon." She wiggles her fingers at us and disappears into the crowd.

"I really feel like she likes me, don't you?" Raven questions.

"She'd be crazy not to."

"Should we be worried about Laney, though? She's harder to read, and I'm wondering if she has doubts about us." Raven's eyes follow where the two women left.

"I don't think you need to worry."

It seems no matter who meets Raven, they are instantly captivated by her. Hell, I know I was.

It was only a matter of time before I could no longer

resist her. I don't think I ever stood a chance. Not since our first meeting at the airport.

"You ready?"

Raven holds the door open to a small boutique tucked away on a bustling arcade full of high-end fashion stores. Herringbone-patterned wood floors gleam under the golden lights. Racks of clothes line the walls. Black cushioned chairs sit at the back of the store.

It screams high-end and fancy.

No doubt out of my budget.

"Ciao. Raven?"

The saleswoman greets us.

"Yes. Marie?"

"Si. A pleasure to meet you both." She sweeps her arm out to us, welcoming us into the store. "I have everything all set up for you. If you have any questions or need different sizes, please let us know."

Her heels click against the floor as we follow her back to the fitting room. Nothing about this store says casual. As we walk, I am captivated by the high-end fabrics, some adorned with pearls and lace.

My mind immediately starts calculating how much everything is going to be. There is no way I can afford anything in this store.

"Stop it." Raven grabs my hand and pulls me closer to her.

"I'm not doing anything."

"Yes, you are. I can hear you thinking from here."

A puff of air leaves me. I'm never not calculating prices in my head.

"I've got this covered," Raven whispers against my ear. It sends shivers racing through me.

I hate how much she affects me. I shouldn't let her get to me, but she is.

"Raven, I don't even know how much these are, but you can't."

"You wouldn't be here if it weren't for me, so there's no argument. Besides,"—a knowing look enters her eyes—"it's as much a gift for me as it is for you."

"What do you mean?"

The hand on my waist dips lower to my hip, squeezing. "It means I can't wait to see you in it. And I can't wait to peel you out of it even more. Now, get your ass in that dressing room."

With a slap to my backside, I scurry into one room and she struts her way toward hers.

I don't know what I'm going to do with her.

Raven

I can't wait to see what Blair is wearing when she comes out of the dressing room. I called ahead to have a few pieces collected for us. I knew if she saw the prices, she'd balk and leave the store.

But with the opera tonight and the gala coming up, I wanted to be sure we both look the part.

And I know whatever Blair wears, she'll look phenomenal.

Zipping up the side of my own black dress, complete with cap sleeves of tulle and a short skirt made of the same fabric, I love how it complements my olive skin. It's the perfect dress for the opera tonight.

Stepping out of the room, I find Blair's door still closed.

"Are you going to show me what you're wearing?" I ask, smoothing a hand down my dress.

"This is too much."

"I'll be the judge of that."

The lock on the door clicks and out comes Blair.

And...wow.

I'm not ready for how gorgeous she looks.

The deep-purple dress is embroidered with darker purple flowers. The strapless, sweetheart neckline highlights every curve of hers. The skirt sweeps out, kissing the ground. Like it's bowing down to her.

"Wow."

"Good wow?"

I nod, my words failing me. I close the distance between us, fingering the soft material.

"Very good wow. Stunning."

"You don't look so bad yourself." Her eyes are focused on the deep V of the front of my dress, dipping between my breasts and showing the top of my stomach.

"Think we'll give those old opera singers a run for their money?"

Blair laughs. "I don't think I'll be able to pay attention to the opera with you sitting there in that."

"Feeling is mutual."

I can't stop touching Blair, fingering the patterns of flowers that seamlessly flow throughout the dress.

Each soft caress has me aching for more.

I didn't even know Blair a week ago, and now she is consuming my every thought. It's never been like this before.

I can't pinpoint why. There's something different about

her. Guarded. Closed off. I want her to open up to me and tell me everything. I want it all with her.

Christ.

And isn't that a problem? When our time together is limited and we'll both go our separate ways.

Hell, I'm paying her to be here.

Except that wasn't on my mind at all last night.

She'll go back to her life, and I'll hopefully have a new company to add to my portfolio.

This doesn't mean anything.

Maybe if I keep telling myself that, I might start to believe it.

Chapter Seventeen

RAVEN

"Is it weird that I'm nervous?" Blair asks, walking up the stairs to the opera house.

"No, because I am too."

"They wouldn't have asked us to get here early if it wasn't a good thing, right?"

"That's what I keep telling myself. God, it's so close I can almost taste it."

"Tonight is going to go off without a hitch. I know it." Blair gives my hand a reassuring squeeze as the doors to the opera are swung open for us.

"Wow. This is stunning." Blair's eyes are wide as she takes in the ornate lobby of the State Opera House.

Waiters are clustered around tables with trays of champagne and canapés. Old portraits hang from the walls. A crystal chandelier hangs down, sending prisms of light through the entire space. Heavy velvets drape through the space, absorbing the sounds of the theater beyond.

It's glittering in its opulence.

But nothing in this places holds a candle to Blair.

"Not as stunning as you." I press a kiss to her neck.

"Stop it."

"I'm serious."

The minute she walked out of that dressing room today in this dress, it took everything I had to keep my hands off her.

Blair doesn't know how sexy she really is. The way her hair curls down one side of her shoulder. The smoky eyeshadow that brings out the blue in her eyes. She saved the purple dress for the final gala and chose a gold dress for tonight. She looks smashing in it. The corset top clings to her curves, and the gold sequins shine in the light. It stops just above her knees, showing off her long legs.

Her neck is bare.

"I forgot to give you this earlier."

I was so blown away by her beauty at the hotel that I had to kiss her. To the point we both needed to reapply our lipstick and then hurry over here.

Opening my clutch, I pull out a small sapphire on a gold chain.

"Raven. I can't accept this."

"You can and you will."

I loop the necklace around her neck and fix the clasp.

It's small, but it reminded me of her. The sapphire captures the blues of her eyes that sweep me away. What I don't tell her is that it was mine. Given to me by my grand-father when I graduated from college.

It's always been my favorite piece, but I want Blair to have it. To see her in this makes my heart swell and butter-flies dance in my stomach.

I'm falling too hard, too fast. But I can't seem to stop myself with her.

For her? I'd give it all up. Everything I've worked for and everything I want just to spend another day with her.

"I don't know what I did to deserve you." Blair pulls

me in for a sweet kiss. Nothing passionate or heated, but it tells me everything I need to know about how she's feeling.

"Sorry, are we interrupting?" Eden pulls my attention away from Blair.

Damn it. The one time I wish she wasn't here.

"Not at all. It's wonderful to see you both." Blair slides right into the gracious person she is, smiling at Eden and Laney. Both of them accept her kisses on the cheek.

"Blair. Raven. I'm thrilled you could join us tonight." Eden looks fabulous in a red ball gown. Laney looks equally stunning in her own strapless black dress.

"I'm glad you were able to organize this. I've never actually been to the opera."

Eden hands Blair and me a glass of champagne each. "You haven't? We love it."

"Do they have the opera in Seattle? I don't know if football fans would enjoy that as much." I laugh.

"Are you football fans?" Laney asks.

"Soccer. But not Raven. I have to drag her to the games back home," Blair responds with a grin.

"Sweaty men running around on a field? Never really been my thing. Now women…" I tell them.

That gets a laugh out of all of them.

"What made you interested in traveLLin'?" Eden asks. "It doesn't really seem to fit in your business portfolio."

Of course she did her due diligence on me. But if she had really dug deep, she would know the types of businesses I help fund.

Small businesses, especially women-owned, are my passion.

"I've been following traveLLin' since I left school. I knew I could travel anywhere as long as they had your seal of approval. Why wouldn't I want to be a part of something so…"

"Life changing," Blair finishes for me. Wrapping an arm around my waist, she pulls me in closer to her. "We still use it to this day when planning our adventures. It's how we planned this trip."

"What's been your favorite part so far?" Eden asks. She carries the conversation while Laney studies us.

The more time we spend with them, the more I learn about them. Eden is the more outgoing of the two while Laney seems to stay in the shadows.

Almost like Blair and me.

"The Duomo. How could it not be?"

"It takes your breath away," Eden says. "I had to include it before leaving Milan behind. Have one last adventure before I turn the company over and explore other parts of the world."

My ears prick up at her words, but I don't let on how much I want this company. I wouldn't be here if I didn't.

"I only wish we had more time to explore," Blair says, regret in her tone.

"Hopefully you'll be able to come back again in the future. Maybe do some scouting?"

"We would love that."

The doors open again, and this time, swarms of people enter.

"Ladies. That's our cue. Enjoy yourselves this evening."

My jaw is on the floor as they greet the rest of the guests.

"Did she say what I think she said? Scouting, like travel locations?" I grasp Blair's arm, needing her to steady me.

"Holy shit. Do you think that means you're in the running?" Blair whispers.

Her eyes are as wide as mine.

"She wouldn't just say something like that to say it, right?"

Blair shakes her head. "A woman like Eden? No. Everything she does is calculated. That's a good thing."

I swallow back the gulp of champagne in my glass, immediately needing another. "Holy shit."

Blair pulls me into her arms, taking me in a fiery kiss. I don't care that we're in a room full of people. I sink my fingers into her hair, letting her control the kiss.

I'm effervescent from the bubbles of champagne, flowing directly into my veins, making me drunk off of her.

"You've got this, Raven. I'm so proud of you." She drops one more peck on my lips before pulling me toward a tray of canapés.

People come and go, greeting us as they mingle with the crowds.

"You know, I hate to say it, but you really are the favorite." Blair nods in the direction of Eden. She looks bored talking to an older man and his husband.

"Are they the ones that go boating every spring?"

"No, those are the ones that own a chain of knitting stores."

I laugh over my drink. "And they want to run traveL-Lin'?" I dismiss Blair with a wave. "No wonder she looks bored."

"Stop it." She elbows me in the side. "I'll have you know I enjoy knitting."

"You do?"

She nods, taking a demure sip of her drink. "It's the one thing I can do where I don't have to focus on anything but what's in front of me."

"Aren't you full of surprises? Maybe you can knit me something."

"Oh yeah?" Blair drops her elbow onto the table, leaning her head against her drawn fist. "Like what?"

"A scarf?"

"And here I thought you'd go for something a little more extravagant."

My eyes sweep up and down her body. "Oh, I'd model it for you. Wearing the scarf, and only that."

She groans, her lashes kissing the tops of her cheeks. "You're just mean."

The overhead lights flicker, indicating it's time to take our seats.

"Guess you'll just have to suffer through for the evening." I throw a wink at her, grabbing her hand and leading her to our private box for the night.

Something I don't mind at all.

We have the perfect view of the stage from here.

"Why is everything so opulent?" Blair traces a finger over the gold, inlaid braiding on the railing of our private box. It's not as extravagant as the lobby. Fresco paintings line the stucco ceilings. Gold coats everything in here, giving it an air of importance. Cushioned red seats make it fit for royalty.

It's everything I'd imagine an opera house to look like.

Sounds are muted this high up. People fill the room, taking their seats before the show starts.

The lights in the hall go down as the curtains open to reveal one lone woman standing on the stage. The high pitch of her voice echoes and stuns everyone into silence.

Her song evokes tragedy and lovesickness and romance all at the same time. I don't have the first clue as to what she's singing about, but it causes a deep yearning inside me.

For the woman sitting next to me.

Is this how the woman felt, pining for her man? Because I'm desperate for Blair, and she's only inches from me.

The show continues, a man now appearing on the stage with her.

"It all sounds so sad," Blair whispers next to me, toying with her new necklace.

"Do you think he broke her heart?" I lean into her, brushing my lips against her ear. I don't miss the way she shudders at the soft touch.

Everything about this woman is mesmerizing. It makes it hard to focus on the stage. Her eyes are filled with the same emotions I'm feeling.

This thing between us started as something fake.

What I apparently don't have to fake?

The feelings I have for Blair.

Turning my attention to the stage, I set my hand on her exposed knee. I drag a finger along her skin.

"What are you doing?" she hisses at me as the singer belts out another morose tune.

Her lover collapses to the stage as she weeps over him.

"They did say to enjoy ourselves."

"I don't think this is what they had in mind." Blair gasps as my hand reaches the heat of her core.

"Yet, I think you want this."

My knuckle grazes the soft fabric of her underwear, already soaked.

"Oh yeah?"

"So damn sexy." Blunt nails dig into my arm, spurring me on. I run my finger past the scrap of material covering her pussy and slide one finger in easily.

"I love that you get so wet for me."

I suck on the pulsing vein in her neck as I work my finger in and out of her at a steady pace. Every time I push back in, she squeezes me harder. Like she doesn't want me to leave her.

"Think you can be quiet?"

Her teeth are digging into her bottom lip. She gives me the smallest of nods. I would've missed it had I not been solely focused on her.

"Good girl."

It's dark in here. With the way the boxes are staggered, no one can see us. The perfect spot for doing naughty things in the dark.

My fingers drag in and out of her, a slow, dizzying pace. Blair spreads her legs, opening her up even farther to me.

"Are you ready?" I tug her earlobe between my teeth.

The music swells around us as Blair whimpers her release. Her head is thrown back in pleasure as I bite down on her shoulder.

Her juices coat my hand as I work her through her release.

She turns a dazed, flushed face to me. "Raven."

Her voice is a prayer. Like she wants to kneel at my altar. I kiss her, pouring as many motions as I can into this.

Voices soften around us as the theater comes back into focus. A woman now lies weeping on the stage.

"Think she died because of an orgasm?" I smile against her cheek.

"I don't think they were doing what we just did back then."

"I should hope not. They wouldn't like us doing this in public."

"You're a bad influence, Raven."

"What can I say? I wanted you to enjoy the opera."

Blair turns a lazy smile on me. Her face is still flushed from coming on my fingers. "I can safely say the opera is my new favorite thing."

I'll sing arias all day long if it means I get to do this with Blair every time.

Thank God for box seats.

Chapter Eighteen

BLAIR

"Where are you taking me?"

"I told you, it's a surprise."

"What if I want to know?" Raven asks.

Hordes of people wearing black and red are pouring out of the metro.

"Can you not guess?"

Darkness has already settled over Milan. Streetlights line the roads leading up to the stadium like a beacon drawing everyone in.

"Soccer match?"

"I believe they call it football here."

"Smart-ass." Raven smirks at me.

"Football. Soccer. Call it whatever you want. This is how we're spending the night."

Our tickets get scanned before I link hands with Raven and wander off to find our seats.

"What makes you think I'll have an issue with how we're spending the night?"

"Are you a soccer fan?"

"Blair, please. It's called football."

"Now who's being a smart-ass…" I lean in for a quick peck.

"Mmm. I don't care how we spend our night as long as I'm spending it with you."

"Careful what you wish for."

I grab two beers from a vendor before strolling through the stadium. The energy around us is palpable.

Soccer fans here are intense on a good day, and I was lucky to find tickets for the game tonight.

With a break coming up soon, I was worried I'd miss them.

Thankfully we didn't. Because while we've been immersed in her world since we arrived, I want to show her a part of my world.

And this is one of the few luxuries I allow myself in my life. When everything I do is for Avi, soccer is mine.

Boos echo around us as a few visiting team fans wander through.

"Is there going to be a fight?" Raven asks, sipping on her beer.

"You worried?"

"I don't know. Should I be?"

"You'll be fine." I can't help but lean in, taking another quick kiss. I love that we can give each other affection here so freely. Now that we've given in to this thing between us, it's easy.

One of the easiest things I've ever done.

"If I tell you I'm not, can I get another kiss?" Raven asks with a grin.

I smile against her lips, loving the taste of beer on her mouth. "Is that the excuse you're going with?"

Raven closes the distance. Her mouth is warm and tantalizing. I want more. So much more.

Someone bumps me from behind, breaking the kiss.

"Can I say I don't like soccer fans?" Raven grumbles.

"C'mon." I laugh, tugging her toward our seats.

"Will you explain the rules to me?" Raven asks.

I give Raven the rundown as both teams walk out onto the field. Milan fans are booing as the opposing team is announced.

"Is it always this loud?" Raven winces.

What I can only assume is the national anthem of Italy starts playing. Everyone is singing passionately at the top of their lungs.

"All the matches I've been to are. At least at home."

The captains shake hands and the game starts. The energy settles as the game progresses.

"How long does it take for someone to score?" Raven's beer is mostly gone as we edge closer to halftime.

"It might not be until extra time."

"And that's…"

"Ninety minutes plus whatever is allowed for stoppage."

Raven's eyes widen. Her cheeks are pink from the cool night air. "Are we going to have to wait that long for them to score?"

"Maybe." I shrug a shoulder.

"And you like this?"

I turn a huge smile on her. "Of course. It's a rush when they score. I love it."

As if on cue, the striker for Milan puts the ball past the goalkeeper, and the crowd goes wild.

"Holy shit!" We both cheer, jumping up with the rest of the fans.

"That was amazing!" Raven is just as happy as I am, even though we have no ties to this team.

Everyone exudes joy as the team piles on top of each other on one end of the field.

"Is it always like that?" Raven nods to where they are.

"Sweaty guys jumping on top of each other?"

"Yeah." Raven loops an arm around my waist, pulling me in close. "You think the women teams do that too when they score?"

I turn, and her face is right there. I drag my nose along her jaw before nipping at her ear. "You sound like you like that idea."

"What if I do?"

I growl as play resumes. "I don't."

"You don't?"

Raven drops into her seat and I follow. "No." I lean closer, not wanting to be overheard, even though it's unlikely given all the exuberant noise ringing through the stadium. "Because I want to be the only sweaty body on top of yours."

Her fingers dig into my knees. Even through the fabric of my jeans, I can feel the sting of her sharp nails. "How can you say that when we have another hour of the game to sit through?"

More like two hours by the time we get back, but I don't tell her that.

"I promise, I'll make it worth your while."

"You better." She squeezes my knee before leaning closer to me.

Wrapping an arm around her, I keep her where she is.

This is what I've missed. With Avi being my entire life, I haven't had the chance to date. I miss a woman's touch. The touch of their lips on mine. The way it feels when they hold me.

It's even better because it's Raven. The attraction that I feel at each touch, each gaze, is something I've never felt before.

God, even out here in the middle of a crowd of thousands, I love feeling her close to me. Raven shouldn't be taking up my every thought, but she is.

With the final event speeding toward us, we'll be heading our separate ways.

"Maybe you can take me to a match at home," Raven tells me as we leave after the game. It ended with a Milan win, 1-0. We link arms as we walk back toward the metro.

"Yeah, sure."

It's wishful thinking. I want us to have more nights like this. Spending time together just the two of us. With no other ulterior motive.

But come this time next week, we'll each go our separate ways. I don't have time in my life with worrying about Avi. She is my entire life. Everything I do is for her. I can't make space for Raven.

It's nice to dream for a little while. That this could be our life.

I blow out a breath as we cram onto the train, wrapping my arms around Raven's waist to hold on tight.

Raven's face is soft as she holds on to the overhead strap.

I'd give anything if this could be our life together…

Anything.

Chapter Nineteen

"I'm surprised so many people came out tonight," Blair yells over the beat of the music.

A few people took Eden up on her offer to come to a dance club in Milan. It sits on a rooftop overlooking the Duomo. Modern tech music blares against the Renaissance architecture.

Old and new.

Milan in a nutshell.

I pour another glass of bubbly, a happy buzz floating through my veins. I'm not sure if it's because of the prosecco or Blair, but it's the perfect night.

Turf lines the floor beneath my stilettos. Lights are strung up as bottles of champagne sit on the tables in the upstairs VIP area that looks out over the rest of the club. The dance floor is crowded as couples of all ages grind against each other. Raised platforms are scattered around the dance floor, with women dancing expertly to the music.

But I'm not paying them much attention as my eyes stay glued to Blair.

She's in a simple pair of dark jeans and a black, silk camisole. It shouldn't look as sexy as it does, but it's Blair.

She could make a paper bag sexy.

"I'm glad you wanted to come." I tuck a loose strand of hair from her ponytail behind her ear, letting my fingers rest against her neck.

"And miss a night out with you? Never."

I replace my fingers with my lips, needing the contact. Blair purrs as I move my lips lower, tasting just how sweet she is.

Her hand settles onto my thigh, squeezing my leg. I put on a pair of short black shorts and a purple sleeveless blouse that leaves very little to the imagination. I didn't miss the way Blair's eyes dipped low as she took in my cleavage before we left the hotel.

I love seeing her so brazen in her perusal of me. I'm just as shameless with her.

I only get Blair for a limited time, and I want to make use of every minute we have together.

"I don't think I ever came to clubs like this in college," I tell her.

"Really?"

I shake my head, sipping on more of my drink. "No. I was always focused on the family business. Even then."

"Well then,"—Blair's eyes light up as she swallows the last dregs of her drink— "we need to change that."

She stands, holding her hand out to me.

"What are we changing?"

"We're dancing. C'mon."

Smiling at her, I finish my drink, setting it on the marbled table in front of me, and take her hand. I pull Blair in for a quick kiss before pushing our way onto the crowded dance floor.

Music thumps through my veins as Blair spins me

around and pulls me into her arms. Bright blue eyes are sparkling with delight as we hold each other close, shaking our hips to the music.

"Maybe if I had someone like you in college to go dancing with, I might have done it more."

Blair smiles, clasping my cheeks before pulling me in for a kiss. It's unhurried. A slow, languid kiss that is the exact opposite of the music.

It's a tasting between the two of us. Enjoying and savoring one another.

My hands drift up her sides, as if memorizing every inch of her luscious body.

"Do you know how sexy you are like this?" Blair pulls me close, lips dancing across the shell of my ear. "All I want to do is get my mouth on you and I can't."

"You don't mean like this?"

I take her in a teasing kiss. Nipping and sucking at her lips. Drinking in the bubbles that she tastes like. I could get drunk off of her.

Bodies sway into us on the dance floor, but I don't care. I don't stop because all I want is Blair. And fuck. I'm not going to be able to wait until we get back to the hotel.

It's like she can read my thoughts as Blair settles a leg between my thighs. Everyone around us is shamelessly dancing.

So what if I start to grind down on Blair, seeking my own relief?

"Just like that, Raven. Yes." Blair's hands creep down my sides, settling over my ass to pull me farther into her. "Think anyone is paying attention to us here?"

My eyes dart around, but no one is looking at us. Other couples are making out. People are smoking cigarettes around the edges of the dance floor. And those closest to the DJ are jumping in the air.

"Fuck. Get me off, Blair."

Her smile is sinful. "With pleasure."

Blair spins us, but not loosening her hold on me. It gives me a better angle as I wrap a leg around her and move against her.

I wish we were naked, but the friction against my clit is sending me soaring.

Every sense is filled with Blair. With the woman who has become so much more than my fake girlfriend.

The way she tastes like the champagne we're both tipsy on. The soft feel of her curves under my fingers. The perfume she wears. The way she sounds when she comes. The way she looks when she's taking in everything around us.

I commit every detail of it to memory as the music fades into the background.

It's only me and Blair. Our lips tangle as I hump her leg. The fabric of her jeans is just what I need, my desire for her amping up.

I love the power Blair holds over me.

"Are you going to come for me, Raven?"

"Yes." My moan is dripping with lust as I throw my head back, the music exploding around us as I come.

"Holy shit."

Blair's lips are sucking on any skin she can find. It's drawing out my pleasure even longer as fire races through me.

I've never felt more free—more wanton—in my entire life. Being with Blair has brought out a new side to me.

Before, everything was about work. I wanted to get ahead. To prove to people that just because I'm a woman doesn't mean I wasn't deserving of taking over the family business.

Now? Now I find myself wanting to make changes. I

don't want to stay at the office for hours on end. I want a life. Someone to go home to.

It's dangerous making these plans with Blair. We've grown closer these last few weeks, but I still feel like there is so much I don't know about her.

Like if she would even want me.

I slump against her, needing the support.

"Do you know how hot you look right now?" Blair trails a single finger down my chest, lingering between my breasts. "You are so sexy, and all I want to do is make you come again."

I'm dripping.

"Then you better get me back to the hotel. Because what I want to do requires fewer clothes."

And giving Blair exactly what she gave me.

Because I'm going to give this woman everything for what little time we have together.

Chapter Twenty

RAVEN

"Why'd Eden change her mind on the final location?" Blair asks, eyes focused on the scenery flying by us out the window. "You never said."

I flip through the magazine I picked up at the train station. It was an early morning after a night at the club. "The whims of the rich, I guess. Wanted to get out of Milan she said."

"Won't they have time to get out of Milan once the gala is over?"

I look at Blair across the small table in the train.

Even in the first class car, there's not that many guests here. It's nice to be able to talk and not worry about crowds of people around us. The rattling of the engine is hypnotic as we speed through the Italian countryside.

It's like the last two weeks with Blair, speeding by. With the final gala this weekend, that's it. We're done.

And the more I think about that, the harder my chest aches.

"Not if they're leaving Italy next week." I go back to

the magazine on the table between us, trying to distract myself from my thoughts.

"Think we'll be able to go out on the water?" Blair drops a hand on top of mine, bringing my awareness solely on her. "Maybe see some famous people?"

"Water, yes. Famous people? No promises." I laugh.

"Damn. And here I thought your name would get us more places."

"I see how it is. Just using me for where I can get you."

"I would never."

"I know." I send a wink her way.

Blair leans back in her seat, kicking her feet up on the chair next to mine. "It's hard to believe that at this time next week, we'll be back in Seattle."

"What's waiting for you back at home?"

Sad blue eyes find mine. "Real life."

"What's so sad about that?"

Blair blows out a breath. "The whole reason I signed up for Elite is to try and earn some extra money to support me and my sister."

The one topic that is off-limits for her. I trace the lines in her palm, watching emotions roil over her face.

I don't press for more, but she gives it to me anyway.

"I'm her legal guardian now."

"You are?" That surprises me.

She nods. "I got kicked out when I was eighteen. My parents were conservative and didn't want me in the house around Avi. Said I would be a bad influence on her. I left for college and never looked back."

"Blair."

"History repeated itself six years later. Avi had a girlfriend at the time. They were at her girlfriend's house and got caught by her parents, and they called ours to tell them. Kicked her out the very next day."

"Fuck."

"Yup. I immediately brought her to live with me."

I cup her hand in mine. "You're kind of incredible, you know that?"

Blair shakes her head. "It's what anyone would have done."

"How old were you?"

"Twenty-four."

"Twenty-four?" I scoff. "I could barely raise myself at that point, and you took in your sister."

"The sad thing is after I got kicked out, I still went to law school. I thought that if maybe I could impress them, even all those years later, they'd welcome me back. Almost as if I could earn their love back."

Standing, I slide over into the seat next to her. "You never should have to earn your parents' love, Blair."

She nods, staring out at the passing countryside en route to Lake Como. There's a tightness in her shoulders that wasn't there before. No wonder she closed this line of questioning on the plane. I wouldn't want to open that old wound.

"Now it's just the two of us. I've moved past it, mostly, but I'm glad that Avi could come be with me. The part that I hate most? Avi having to go through it."

"I'm sorry that happened to you." I cup her cheek, dropping my forehead to hers. "They don't deserve someone as wonderful as you."

I want to do nothing but shower Blair in love. Having gone through so much and being the wonderful woman that she is, she deserves it.

"I hope you know how incredible you are," I whisper against her lips. She shakes her head, but I stop her. "No, you are. I'm in awe of you. I don't know if I would've been able to do what you're doing."

Everything clicks. Why she's in a job she hates trying to support her sister. I want to do everything I can to help her. Not that she'll let me. She has too much pride for that.

But I'll damn well try.

"Raising a teenage girl is not easy," Blair laughs, breaking the tension.

"God, I remember how I was at her age. I think I still had a boyfriend then."

"Was that the first boy you ever made cry?"

"Stop it." I poke her in the side. "But yes. When he tried to feel me up, I kicked him in the balls and realized I liked girls."

Blair pulls my arm around her shoulders and snuggles into my side. "Been making the boys cry ever since."

"And the women just as happy."

"That I can confirm."

Something I realize I want to do way past this trip.

I've gone and fallen for Blair Stevens.

Turns out all I needed was a shove from the universe to finally take Gram's advice.

Chapter Twenty-One

BLAIR

"I can't get over how beautiful it is here."

"Not as beautiful as you," Raven whispers into my hair, keeping me close.

"You don't have to lay it on so thick," I laugh.

If possible, the streets are even more crowded here than Milan. Every sidewalk café is filled to the brim. Wine is flowing as people enjoy their summer holiday. Boats are zipping across the lake.

"It's true."

"Stop it."

"Hey." Raven draws me up short of our intended destination. "I am going to tell you as often as I can, while I can, because it's the truth. You're one of the most beautiful women I've ever met. Inside and out. So you better get used to this."

I can't help the smile that spreads across my face. Things have been different since I told her about Avi on the train yesterday.

Freeing. Like I don't have to hold anything back. I want to show her how I truly feel about her.

Because there's only a handful of people in my life I've told about Avi. The ones that have to know.

I wanted to tell Raven. Every wall I had up, she climbed right past and knocked over on her way up.

"Is that okay with you?" Raven's smile now matches mine.

"I suppose."

"Good." She gives me a quick kiss before pulling me between the trees. "Now can I give you your surprise?"

Wooden posts bursting with flower baskets line the rickety pier as we walk toward the waiting boat. "A boat ride?"

When Raven told me the location change for the final gala the other night, I was hesitant at first. But seeing Lake Como? Getting to come to one of the most beautiful places in the world?

I don't know why I thought twice. Maybe because I like our little bubble in Milan.

"You can't come to Lake Como and not experience the lake." Raven smiles, no doubt her eyes lit up behind her dark sunglasses.

"Ciao signorina y signorina," the boat captain greets us. "A beautiful day, no?"

"Gorgeous. Thank you for taking us on such short notice."

He nods, sweeping out his arm to allow us on the boat.

It's small, but there's a wide, open deck with bench seats, covered in navy-and-white striped cushions. Stairs disappear to a small kitchen below deck.

A table, complete with a full breakfast spread, is set at the stern of the boat.

"Wow. This is quite the setup."

Croissants. Fruit. Meats. Cheeses. A bottle of Prosecco.

"Make yourselves comfortable and let me know if you

need anything." The captain nods before taking the stairs up to his spot.

"Grazie." Raven smiles at him. "You know, I have a lot of good ideas, but this might be my best yet."

"Wow. Ever the humble woman."

"Hey." Raven elbows me as she pops the bottle of Prosecco. "This deserves it."

The captain starts the engine, and we head out into the lake, away from the shore.

"You're right. I will give you that." Grabbing a piece of cheese, I pop it into my mouth as Raven pours us each a hearty flute of bubbly.

"Thank you." I accept it with a huge smile on my face.

"Saluti." Raven clinks her glass against mine.

"Cheers."

We enjoy a quiet breakfast as we head toward the other side of the lake. Everything about this place is stunning.

Deep blue and turquoise water shimmers in the sunlight. Terra-cotta-colored buildings line the mountains around the lake. The bright blooms of flowers can be seen even from the middle of the lake.

With the cool breeze blowing through, it's perfect.

Everything about this day is perfect.

Because I'm sitting here with Raven.

"Thinking pretty hard, Blair," she whispers in my ear. Raven wraps an arm around my shoulders, pulling me into her side.

"It's hard to believe I'm here."

"You deserve the world, Blair. I want to be the person to give it to you."

It's easy to get wrapped up in this, thinking that this could be our every day together.

Except it won't be. We only have a few more days here.

With the final gala here tomorrow night, our time in Italy is almost over.

As easy as our time is here, it won't last. No woman has ever fit into my life. They take one look at Avi and run the other direction. Not that I blame them. Who would sign up to help me raise a sixteen-year-old?

Besides, Raven will have her new company to manage. I'm sure of it. She wouldn't have time for us. Better to be let down now than in six months when she won't be bothered to give up her job for us.

No. It's better this way.

"C'mon. Let's go lay out."

I need to cut off these thoughts. Grabbing Raven's hand and the drinks, I lead us out onto the main deck.

It's hot, the perfect temperature for a dip in the lake. Raven drops her cover-up, and every thought of mine is consumed by her.

How is it possible to be jealous of a swimsuit? The way it clings to her like a second skin has my thighs clenching.

"You okay there?"

I straddle Raven's legs, dragging a finger along the hem of her suit.

"Mmm. Just enjoying the sights."

"I think you're missing them." Raven threads her fingers through my hair, pulling me close.

"I don't think I am."

I couldn't care less about the view in front of us. All I want is Raven. I kiss her. Slow, lazy, languid. Letting our tongues tangle as the wind whips our hair around.

It's a decadent morning spent with Raven.

"Would you like to swim?" the captain interrupts.

I groan, but Raven's eyes light up.

"Yes!" She pushes me to the side and runs to back of the boat. I take off after her, not a care in the world.

She goes flying in and I go right after her.

"Fuck! It's freezing!" It's like a thousand tiny needles are stabbing my skin.

"It's not that bad." She wipes the water from her eyes.

"Not that bad? My nipples could cut glass."

A devilish look crosses her lips as she swims over to me.

"Do you need me to check?"

One hand wraps around my waist as the other slides up my swimsuit-clad body. Her thumb strokes over my already hard nipple.

"Mmm."

The smallest touch has me arching into her.

"You know we're not alone out here, right?" A shiver leaves me, even though I can feel Raven's warmth start to seep into me.

"What a shame." Her mouth nips at my jaw. "What I wouldn't give to have this lake all to ourselves."

"I don't think there's enough money in the world for that."

"Settle for a kiss then?"

Warm lips take mine in a commanding kiss. Any thought of being cold is gone.

The swipe of her tongue into my mouth has me aching for her. A feeling low in my belly stirs, craving everything she'll give me. Her skin is cold as I dig my fingers into her, both of us holding on to each other as best we can in the water.

Wandering hands slip under the bottom of my top.

"Raven..." I tug her bottom lip between my teeth as she pushes her hand farther under my top, cupping my breast.

"Who has the power now?"

"God, you. You do." I throw my head back as she kneads my breast. I wish we weren't out in the middle of this lake right now. I'd rather be spread out beneath her and letting her feast on me.

"That's right." She licks a trail up my neck. "I love seeing how crazy I can make you."

"You're just mean."

"I am?" She nibbles on my jaw, squeezing a little bit harder. I can feel her smile in it.

"Yes. I want to be naked. Under you. Every which way you'll have me, but instead we're in the middle of a lake."

"Now you're giving me ideas for later." Raven pulls her hand back and swims away from me a little bit. "I think I'll wait until then."

"Are you kidding me?"

Every nerve is on fire. Each part of me is yearning for her touch. For her fingers to be back where they were.

"It'll just make it that much better."

I splash her. "No, it won't."

"Now you're being mean," she returns, sweeping both arms through the water to hit me.

The cold water now helps cool the raging heat swirling through me as we splash each other. The moment goes from heated to playful in the blink of an eye.

Something I love about Raven.

Shit. Love?

There's no way I could love her in this short of a time. But her bright eyes looking back at me, reflecting so much happiness, tell me otherwise.

I've gone and fallen in love with Raven West.

Now, how do I keep her past this week?

Because now that I've had her, I never want to let her go.

Chapter Twenty-Two

BLAIR

Why am I so nervous? This is going to be a piece of cake. From everything I've witnessed since we arrived in Milan, Eden loves Raven. So why wouldn't she sell her the company?

Swiping the last of my lip gloss over my lips, I give myself a once-over in the mirror.

The purple dress is stunning. I'm glad I saved this one for tonight. I've never felt so beautiful in my entire life.

I keep waiting for all of this to unravel. For me to say something stupid and let the cat out of the bag that this is all fake.

But is it?

My feelings toward Raven are anything but fake. Every touch, every glance. All of it feels very, *very* real. And the thought of this ending?

It has my heart squeezing in my chest.

"Are you ready, Blair?" Raven's voice calls from the bedroom, breaking me out of my thoughts.

"One second."

Butterflies are threatening to explode out of me. I want

everything to be perfect tonight for Raven. I've seen the work she puts into her job. The love and care. She deserves to be the new owner of traveLLin'.

Taking one last steady breath, I step out of the bathroom and am stunned speechless.

Raven is hands down one of the sexiest people I've ever seen in my life. But tonight? Tonight, she takes my breath away.

The black dress clings to her every curve. The short length shows off her long legs, and the way it dips between her cleavage has me drooling.

"Wow."

"You like?" She does a spin in those same red-soled heels that I love seeing her in.

"Like?" I close the distance between us. "I love."

Every strand of hair is perfectly coiffed into place, a fun and sexy fauxhawk to go with the vibe of the event tonight.

"You don't look so bad yourself."

She wraps her arms around my purple dress, pulling me in close.

"I have to say, you were right."

"Yeah?" Raven quirks a perfectly manicured brow at me.

"This dress really is incredible."

She leans in closer, pressing a kiss to the corner of my mouth. "And it will look even better on the floor tonight."

My fingers dig into her arms as I turn my head to capture her lips.

I want every piece of Raven West.

How is it that a fake relationship could turn out to be the most real thing in my life?

"We really don't have time for this." Raven is breathless as she pulls her mouth away from mine. "We can't be late."

"Is anyone really on time to a big event like this?" I wipe the smeared lipstick from her mouth.

"When there will likely be a big entrance by Eden and Laney? Yes."

I fight a groan. This is everything the two of us have been working toward. I want it for Raven almost as much as she does.

"Only a few hours, Blair. I promise."

Latching our hands together, we make the short walk from the hotel to the villa.

The grand palace is lit up on the outside, welcoming everyone here. The gardens are in full bloom as music thrums through the space.

It's the place to be tonight.

"Before we go in…" Raven stops, pulling me back into her. Her fingers toy with the necklace she gave me. Something I don't know I'll ever be able to take off.

"You okay?"

"Thank you."

"For what?"

"For being here with me."

"It's the whole reason I'm here." Maybe if I keep reminding myself of it, I'll start to believe it.

Because she's the reason I'm here. Not for some sale of a company. Her. Raven. I would do anything for her.

And tonight? That's to help her win this bid.

I slip my mask into place, watching as she does the same.

"Right. Well…thanks anyway."

I want to tell her that I'm not here for the reasons she thinks I am anymore. That over the last few weeks I've fallen for her. The person that she is, not the one she shows the world.

But I can't.

Because as soon as we land in Seattle on Monday, this thing is over.

We're done. My contracted time with her is up.

And that thought pains me more than I can ever tell her.

"Thank you, everyone, for being here tonight," Eden welcomes us. "I can't tell you what your being here these last few weeks has meant to me. It's been a pleasure getting to know all of you."

"Holy shit. Is she doing it now?" Raven whispers next to me.

"I think she might be."

Raven grabs my hand and holds tight.

"TraveLLin' is my baby. While Laney and I never had children, I nurtured this company into what it is today. That's why it's been so hard for me to hand over the reins. And why I wanted to make sure I was giving it to the right person."

Murmurs break out in the crowd. The energy is high. This is what everyone has been working toward while we've been here.

And it all comes down to one person.

"All of you have a vision and would do well to lead this company. But there is one person who has truly shone these last few weeks."

"I think I'm going to be sick." Raven drops her head on my shoulder.

"Raven West," Eden's voice booms. "I am thrilled to be the one to tell you that West Investments has won the bid for traveLLin'."

"You did it!"

"She said my name?" Raven is in shock. "That was my name, right?"

"Babe, you did it!" Cupping her jaw, I drop kisses all over her face.

"Raven, if you'll join me on stage."

"Go!" I shove her toward the stage, wanting her to have her moment.

People swarm her, pushing me to the side.

She's swallowed up by the crowd, and it's in that moment, I know I've lost her. This was Raven's goal. And now that she's got it?

I'm no longer needed.

Chapter Twenty-Three

RAVEN

"Eden, I can't thank you enough."

"Raven, you really were the only person right for it."

Since Eden said my name on the stage, I've been in a state of shock. As soon as I was pushed toward the stage, I lost track of Blair.

A moment this big deserves to be celebrated with the ones you love.

Now that I have traveLLin', I want Blair too. There's nothing stopping us. I want to have a life with her. With her and her sister.

Finding Laney by the bar, I grab her.

"Have you seen Blair?"

"She said she wasn't feeling well and was going to go back to the hotel."

"Wait, she left?"

"About twenty minutes ago. And if I were you, I wouldn't let that woman get away."

Her comment draws me up short. "I'm sorry?"

Eden approaches the two of us, my nerves now starting to come back in full force.

"Do you really think we're that dumb?" Laney laughs. "It was all a ruse between the two of you. You're not the only ones that did their due diligence."

"But…" My mouth goes dry.

"We did our research on you. You're a force to be reckoned with, Raven. But you reminded me of me when I first started this business. No attachments to anyone. You had a quote in an article with the Seattle Star a few months back about how you've been single for so long it makes it easier to run the business."

That damn article I did a few months back. I used to wear my singlehood like a badge of honor. Not wanting or needing anyone in my life. Turns out, finding the *right* partner makes all the difference.

"But then we saw you two together. Reminded me of the two of us." Eden's face is soft as she looks at Laney. "No one could pull me away from work like she could. The same way I saw Blair pull you away."

"You knew it was fake? And you're still giving me your company?"

Eden nods, but Laney is the one who speaks. "While you were trying to impress Eden, it let me observe you two. It was subtle, but it was there."

"And you still trust me with your company?" After all that, to lose what I came here for would be devastating.

But would it be as devastating as losing Blair?

Laney takes my hand in hers. "Getting to watch the two of you fall in love? You can't witness anything greater than that."

"Besides," Eden interjects, "the two of you running this company together? You'll be the balance each other needs to make it work."

I blow out a breath. "I'm sorry for lying."

Eden waves me off. "Are you really? Even though you fell in love?"

"I guess not."

"Now, why are you standing around talking to us? Go get your girl."

"Thank you. Truly."

Dropping kisses on each of their cheeks, I head off in the direction we came from. There is no way I'm letting Blair run scared. Not with everything finally within reach.

This was never meant to be fake. It's the most real thing in my life, and I won't stop until I'm back in her arms.

Kicking out of my heels, I pick them up and run along the promenade back to the hotel.

Only I don't make it far.

Blair is standing about fifty feet away, a lone light casting her shadow on the path.

"Were you going to leave without saying goodbye?" I call out to her.

She startles, turning to face me. Tears wet her eyes.

"You got what we came for."

"Not everything."

"You sealed the deal."

"The company, yes. But there's one more thing I want."

"What's that?"

Blair doesn't look at me as I close the distance between the two of us. "You."

She stiffens, goose bumps breaking out across her skin.

"But…it was all for show."

"Was it?" I sweep a blonde lock of hair back off her shoulder.

"Uh-huh." Her voice stutters.

"Are you sure about that?"

Her eyes close, like she's willing herself to have this conversation with me.

"Why would it be anything else, Raven?" Her voice is quiet.

"It was a lot more for me."

"It was?" Her gaze snaps up to meet mine. Blue eyes, full of hope, are staring into mine.

Resting my hands on her hips, I turn her to face me. The wind off the lake blows around us.

"It might've started out fake, Blair, but it's not for me anymore. Not for a long while. Somewhere along the way, I fell in love with you. Even Eden and Laney could see it."

"They knew?" She gasps.

"They knew. And they still gave me their company."

She bites down on the corner of her lip, eyes welling with tears.

"I don't open myself up to anyone. A downside of the business I'm in. You were the exception."

"Yeah?"

"The only one. The only person who ever even bothered to try." Cupping her cheek, I tug her lip free from the clutches of her teeth. "I don't want anyone but you, Blair. You're it for me."

"Really? Because my life isn't exactly easy right now. I have my sister to think about, and we're a package deal."

"I know."

"And my job doesn't really make it conducive to being in a new relationship and—"

I cut her off by sealing my lips over hers. She melts into my touch.

This. This is why I love her. She never thinks about herself. I want to be the one to put her first.

Not my business or traveLLin'. Her. Only her.

"I'm going to need someone I trust to help run traveLLin'."

"Me? Really?"

"You'd be incredible. With your skills and drive? We'll be taking over the world."

She huffs out a laugh. Warm hands drift around my waist, holding me close. "Do you think I'd be able to steal you away from work? Visit some of these places we talk about?"

"Remote beaches with you? A drink in hand? Can we go right now?"

Blair presses a kiss to the corner of my mouth. "I'd go anywhere with you, Raven."

"Does this mean you'll stay?"

She nods against me. "As long as you won't be hiring out any more girlfriends for company functions."

This woman. She drives me mad sometimes, but I wouldn't have it any other way.

"Then maybe I should think about upgrading that title of yours from fake girlfriend."

"To what?" Blair takes my extended hand, linking our fingers together.

"Partner. On a permanent basis."

"Yeah?" Her breath leaves her in a rush. "You'd want that?"

I nod, pulling her into me and wrapping my arms around her waist. "I want everything with you, Blair. The good, the bad, the ugly."

"There might be a lot of ugly. I have a teenager after all." She drops her forehead to mine.

"It's what we do for love, Blair. I love you. And I know I'll love Avi just as much."

"I love you, Raven." Blair closes the distance between

the two of us, connecting our mouths. Sealing the promise we made to one another.

"I'm sure my Gram will be happy to know that I'm as happy as she is," I laugh against her cheek.

"I can't wait to meet her."

"You'll love her."

Blair shakes her head. "Not as much as I love you."

She seals it with a kiss. The best kiss of my life.

Because it's with the woman I truly love.

Blair Stevens.

My fake girlfriend.

The most real person I've ever met and fallen in love with.

Thank God for Elite.

Epilogue

BLAIR - SEVENTEEN MONTHS LATER

"I've got Dick's!"

Avi's voice carries through the house, the back door slamming shut.

"Is that joke ever going to get old?" I ask, grabbing the bag of burgers from Avi. The smell of grease and fries overwhelms me.

Absolutely delicious.

"Nope." She sucks her milkshake dry. "Maybe it'll prove useful to scare off any boys."

"Are we scaring off boys now?" Raven strides into the kitchen, grabbing her shake from the cardboard container. She drops a peck on my cheek.

Now that we're living together, Raven is home early most days, splitting the parenting responsibilities with me.

"Ugh. Don't even put that out into the universe. I don't want to deal with you and a guy," Blair whines.

"Would it be better if it were a girl?"

"Yes," Raven and I answer at the same time.

"God, you two are disgustingly cute."

Avi grabs the bag and walks into the dining room.

My eyes rove over Raven. She looks relaxed in black leggings and a pink camisole. With the cold weather settling in, a gray cardigan hangs off her shoulder.

Some days, I still have to pinch myself that this is my life now. I never thought I would be so lucky to find someone like Raven.

She loves me more than I ever thought possible. And me? I'd die for her.

A few months ago, Avi and I moved into her house with her. It's cozy now with the three of us, but with the finished basement, Avi has her own space.

I was worried about how our lives would blend, but it's been seamless. Avi loves Raven.

Which means less of a load on me. Avi is looking at colleges, and I no longer have to worry about how I'm going to pay for it.

With the pay raise that came with running traveLLin', I can contribute in a meaningful way to our relationship. No more sticking with a career I don't love to impress people who don't matter.

I have my people. Raven. Avi. Sarina. Raven's family.

I wouldn't trade anything for our life we have together.

"Don't forget you have that calculus test tomorrow." Raven drops a kiss on Avi's head as she takes her seat.

"Quiz me. I know it all." Avi has a smart-ass look on her face.

Raven bursts out laughing, grabbing her own dinner. "I wouldn't know the first thing to quiz you on."

"Maybe I should teach you then."

"Hell no. You could not pay me enough. Maybe I'll have Chelsea help you study."

"Your assistant knows calculus?" I ask.

"I'll pay her to learn calculus so we don't have to."

Avi pops a fry into her mouth. "Can I pay her to take my English test on Friday?"

"Or," I cut off any further argument from Avi and ideas of paying people to study for her, "you do the work, and once school is out for holiday break, you can relax on the beach in Saint Lucia."

"Is that where we're going?" Excitement oozes from her.

"I thought we were telling her tomorrow?" Raven looks over her milkshake at me.

"Consider it incentive to study."

"I promise I'll get an A."

Our time over the Christmas holiday is split. I plan a trip for traveLLin', and we visit Raven's family on the rest of the break.

It's one of the things that I love most. Not only did I get Raven, but we were accepted with open arms into her family. They love Avi and spoil her rotten.

She and Gram are thick as thieves.

I couldn't have asked for anything more.

"You better. Otherwise you won't go ice fishing with Grandpa," Raven tells her. "He has a new spot he wants to take you to."

"But only if you pass your test."

"Which means you need to study."

Avi's eyes flit between the two of us. "Do you two practice this when I'm not around?"

"No," we answer in sync.

"You're disgustingly cute. You should just get married already!" Avi grabs the last burger and heads downstairs to her room.

"Avi!" I yell after her. "You can't stay stuff like that."

"What? It's true."

She disappears down the stairs, and I'm left shaking my head at her.

"She's got a point." Raven sips on her shake, pulling me into the living room on the oversized couch. The fire is crackling on this dark night. It's the perfect romantic night —and we are lucky enough to get one every night.

"Is this you proposing?" I roll my eyes and grab her shake and finish it off.

"By saying your sister has a point? Please."

"Oh yeah? Then how would you do it?"

I'm egging her on. I know this. But I don't care. We've talked about getting married before, but the two of us are content. Happy.

Neither of us need a label.

"I would tell you how much I love you. How I never imagined you coming into my life the way you did."

"I've heard all of this before."

Except it doesn't cut through the buzzing that's now coursing through my veins. Something about this time feels different.

"And do you ever get tired of hearing it?" Raven pulls me over her on the couch. I wrap my arms around her shoulders, until we're impossibly close.

"No."

"I love how you love me. How you love your sister. Your drive and dedication."

Her hands drift up my thighs, squeezing my hips.

"What you've done not only for me, but for her... We're lucky to have you. Everyone who meets you is lucky to know you. You're compassionate and warm and so damn wonderful, I don't know what I would do without you."

"What are you saying?" My breath is a whisper against her lips.

"Marry me, Blair. I love you so damn much that I don't want to spend another minute not tied to you for the rest of my life."

"Yeah?"

Raven drags her nose along mine. "Yeah. I want the label. I want you to be my wife. No more dicking around."

A watery laugh escapes me. "Had to go with a dicking joke in your proposal?"

"Would you expect anything less?"

Soft brown eyes are staring at me. It's one of the things I love most about her. I can read her like an open book where others can't. I'm one of the only people that gets to see this side of her.

Just me.

"Will you say yes already?!" Avi shouts from the basement.

"Have you been eavesdropping this whole time?" I pull back from Raven as Avi bounces into the living room.

"Yes! Raven asked my permission last week."

"You did?" My eyes snap back to the woman who has won both of us over.

She nods. "I had to make sure she likes me."

"Please. I love you, Raven. And I want you and Blair to get married."

"So, what do you say, Blair? Want to get married?"

A smile I couldn't even hope to contain breaks out. "On one condition."

"What might that be?"

I tuck a lock of black hair behind her ear.

"Can we do it in Saint Lucia? No time like the present, right?"

Raven smirks. "I've already booked flights and hotels for everyone."

"It's a yes?" Avi asks.

"Yes!" I shout, being wrapped in hugs from my two favorite people.

"I'm going to go call and tell everyone I know." Avi drops a kiss on my cheek and runs off.

"Is that her way of being scarce tonight?" Raven whispers as the basement door slams shut behind her.

"I'm not complaining."

I capture her lips with mine, pouring everything I'm feeling into this kiss. I love everything she shows me every day. I never thought this kind of life would be possible.

"Do I get a ring?" A few stray tears escape.

"It's at the office. I didn't think I'd do it tonight, but…"

"But Avi was impatient," I laugh. "Still want the two of us?"

Raven clasps my face in her hands. "Both of you. I love you, Blair. So damn much, I think my heart might explode."

"Let's not hope for that. Because you're all I need."

"Everything," she whispers.

"A family."

What I've always wanted, I found with Raven.

The woman who hired me to be her fake girlfriend. She gave me everything my life was missing.

With Raven by my side, I feel like the most powerful woman in the world.

Bonus Epilogue

"Do we really have to go home tomorrow?"

"You know we have to get back to real life," Blair tells me, dropping a kiss onto my sun-kissed skin. "We both have meetings—"

"Shush." I cut her off. "No talk of meetings. Not on our honeymoon."

"You know, just because we're going home doesn't mean the honeymoon is over."

Shifting on the lounger of our private cabana, I shield my eyes from the hot sun. Belize has been an absolute dream. We've had a few tours we've gone on, but most of our time has been spent in our over-the-water hut at the end of the dock.

I take in my new wife. Blair looks perfect out here – blissful, tan and utterly relaxed.

I love seeing her like this.

It's crazy because it feels like nothing has changed.

We were already living together. Already raising Avi—with the added exception of hunting for colleges for her to attend. Both working our busy jobs.

Spending our nights wrapped around each other.

Except…everything has changed.

We're linked together forever now. Something I've wanted since pretty much the day I met her.

Blair is the one person I share everything with. She's a true partner and my best friend in the entire world. Everything I do, I do for the three of us.

"Do you think we can make use of the rest of our time here?"

I crawl over toward her on the large lounger.

Blair rests against the back of the chair, taking me in. "What did you have in mind?"

Pulling Blair closer to me, she splays out beneath me. I press a kiss to the inside of her knee.

"What I plan to do is devour *my wife*."

"Mmm." Blair squirms underneath me. "I don't know if I'll ever get used to hearing you call me that."

I lick a path up to the bottoms of her swimsuit, tugging at the material with my teeth. "My wife. Only mine."

I nibble at her hips. Suck on the soft skin of her stomach. Throwing a leg over her, I stare down at her beautiful body.

"How did I get so lucky?" I trace a finger along the cup of her green swimsuit. The two-piece doesn't cover much. As she said, she wanted to cover the important bits while laying in the sun.

Finding the ties of the triangles, I pull the fabric loose. Her nipples are already tight. Hard.

"I guess you picked the right woman."

"And right now, I'm going to take the power back."

I love that Blair showers me with attention in the bedroom. She gets me out of my head, always putting me and my needs first. With her, I never fail to come multiple times.

And now, I'm going to be giving her that attention. Because she deserves it.

"I love seeing you like this."

Swirling my fingertip around the tight bud, I play with her. Goosebumps break out across her skin. I tweak it. Tug it. Blair is arching into my touch.

"Fuck, Raven. I need your mouth."

"Oh yeah?" I close the distance between the two us, giving her a light, teasing kiss.

"Not there." Blair clasps my cheeks between her hands and forces my head lower. "Here."

I'm hovering above her breasts now. They are ripe for the taking. A sly smile spreads across my face as I press a kiss to her cleavage.

"Not yet, my love."

I pepper every part of her skin with kisses except for where she really wants me. Her moans and whimpers tell me it's driving her mad.

"God, Raven."

"Yes?" I rest my head on my hand, leaning on my elbow. The sun glints off her body, making her look like an angel.

"Fucking eat me out."

"Don't like it when you're being teased?"

She perks up on her elbows. "Is this how I make you feel?"

"Every time."

"It's not nice to make your wife wait," Blair tells me.

I shift back onto my knees between her legs. "I guess I could put you out of your misery." Except I don't. Not immediately. My hands take their time as they untie the sides of her bikini bottoms. Peeling the material off her, I toss it behind me. It lands on the deck with a wet smack.

Grabbing her legs, I push them wider, opening her up

to me. It's glistening in the sunshine and I can't wait to have my way with it. "Your pussy is perfect. So fucking perfect like this."

I drag my tongue between her folds. She's already wet. I love tasting her like this.

Delicious. Sweet. Sublime.

"Fuck." Blair's hands find my hair, holding tight. "More."

This time, I give her what she wants. I bury my face between her legs. Flicking and sucking on her clit. Amping up her own need. Every sound that hits my ears makes me wet. I'm practically humping the lounger below me as I eat Blair out.

"Oh my god. I'm going to come!" Blair shouts.

I push two fingers inside her and hook them toward me. It sends her over the edge. Blair's thighs squeeze my head and I drink in every drop of her release. It feels endless.

"God, Raven." The pressure against my ears lessens as Blair slumps back. "Why is it always so good?"

"Because it's us." I lick the remains of her orgasm off my lips.

"My turn." Blair pulls me up her sated body and flips us over. Her mouth is greedy as she steals a kiss from me. I let her take command as her tongue swipes against mine.

Blair's hands wander down my body, stripping me naked. She thrusts two fingers inside, eliciting a gasp from me.

I grind down on her fingers, seeking my own pleasure. Blair knows exactly how to get me there.

"C'mon, Raven. Come apart for me."

Blair sucks on the tender skin on my neck as her thumb connects with my clit. It's the softest touch, but I'm already on edge from making her come. It's enough to push me over the cliff into an endless abyss of pleasure.

"Blair!" I shout, riding her hand.

"That's it. Give it all to me."

My skin feels too tight for my body as I ride the high of my pleasure. It's a feeling I'll never get over as Blair holds me in her arms.

I don't know if it's the emotion from our honeymoon, our wedding or the sheer amount of love I have for Blair, but it has tears wetting my eyes.

"What's wrong?" Blair looks concerned now.

"Promise me."

"What?" Blair traces her thumb across my lips. "Anything. You know I'll give you anything."

"We never stop doing this. No matter how old and gray we get, that we'll always do this."

"Have sex?" Blair asks.

"Taking trips. Making time for each other. Never losing this spark we have now."

A tender smile spreads across Blair's face. "Never. We will never stop doing this."

And she seals her promise with a kiss.

Reaching out to Elite Connections was one of the best decisions I've ever made. Because it gave me Blair.

It gave me the life I've always dreamed of.

And I wouldn't trade it for the world.

Author's Note

BOOK NUMBER TWENTY-TWO IS OUT IN THE WORLD!

It's hard to believe this is book #22. I love that I was included in the Elite Connections Anthology — this book raised $10,000 for charity! How incredible is that?! I love the book world. Writing inclusive love stories is one of my favorite things about being author, and I'm so thankful that I get to tell these stories that hopefully people can see themselves in.

There are so many people I want to thank. Ashli and Rhys for allowing me to write this story to start with — it was one of the best experiences I've had as an author! Thank you to Jodi and Ashlee for beta reading this book for me. To all my incredible author friends, who are too many to name here. You know I love you!

To my Street Team and the Silver Society…I love getting to share my books with you and your excitement for them. Thank you to all the readers everywhere…for sharing and loving on my books and characters! There aren't enough words to thank you for your support!

<3 Emily

Also by Emily Silver

Colorado Black Diamonds Hockey

Best Kept Secret

Best Laid Plans

Best of the Best

Best of Both Worlds - coming October 31

Dixon Creek Ranch

Yours to Take

Yours to Hold

Yours to Be

Yours to Forget

Yours To Lose

Yours To Love - a newsletter freebie

The Denver Mountain Lions

Roughing The Kicker

Pass Interference

Sideline Infraction

Illegal Contact

The Big Game

Standalones

Off the Deep End

The Highland Escape

Merry in Moose Falls - coming November 21

The Ainsworth Royals

Royal Reckoning

Reckless Royal

Royal Relations

Royal Roots

Royal Ties

The Love Abroad Series

An Icy Infatuation

A French Fling

A Sydney Surprise

Love Under An Italian Sky

Get the trope guide on my website, or
scan the QR code to read my books now!

About the Author

After winning a Young Author's Award in second grade, Emily Silver was destined to be a writer. She loves writing inclusive stories, with strong heroines and the swoony men who fall for them.

A lover of all things romance, Emily started writing books set in her favorite places around the world. As an avid traveler, she's been to all seven continents and sailed around the globe.

When she's not writing, Emily can be found sipping cocktails on her porch, reading all the romance she can get her hands on and planning her next big adventure!

Find her on social media to stay up to date on all her adventures and upcoming releases!

www.ingramcontent.com/pod-product-compliance
Lightning Source LLC
Chambersburg PA
CBHW030141010826
48973CB00002B/663